SHARING HER

CANDY QUINN

PATHFORGERS PUBLISHING

Book Themes:

MFM, virginity, breeding, billionaire, BDSM

Word Count:

54,067

Newsletter:

Sign up here for a free, exclusive & taboo novella: http://candyquinn.com/newsletter/

BUYING HER

I bite my lip and feel heat ripple up my stomach as my fingers rub the swollen little nub between my legs. It's only been a few minutes, but my pussy is already on fire.

I'm lying on the fluffy blanket of my bed, naked except for a thin white t-shirt, and there's no light in the room except for the glow of the screen sitting next to me.

My gleaming blue eyes are glued to the video playing on the screen.

On it, a girl who looks just like me is getting pounded from behind by one guy who had to be at least 6'6", and her mouth is full of another guy's cock that looks so thick and long that I can't believe she isn't choking. I'm only halfway through the first video, and I'm already so close. My cheeks burn. I'm so ashamed of myself.

But for as long as I can remember, nothing has been hotter to me than the idea of two guys having their way with me.

The girl in the video looks so much like me it's scary. She can't be over 18, and her long red hair is cut the same way mine is. When the guy behind her squeezes her ass, I reach behind me to touch mine and imagine him doing the same thing. When her full lips take more of that monster cock into her mouth, I lick my lips and imagine myself taking it all in just like her.

When the guys start to groan, getting close to release, it's just too much for me. I feel my muscles tightening as I squirm on the bed, and the orgasm starts to boil up out of nowhere. My toes curl, and I push my free hand under my shirt to start playing with my tits while the little circles I'm making with my fingers on my clit get faster and faster. My mouth falls open, and the thought of some hung college hunk shoving his cock into it pushes me right over the edge.

I squeal as I come, and it its me so hard I close my legs and roll to the side while I massage myself. I make a big mess all over my hands, but the groans of the guys on screen carry me through the orgasm like they're really there. I crack my eyes open in time to watch her face get covered in hot, white cream, and I lick my lips, wishing it was there for me to drink up for real.

I'm a good girl. Perfect grades, always studying, never in trouble. But I want to be a good girl for someone different.

And now, I finally have my chance.

My dorm room door flies open, and I squeal, throwing the covers over my body and slamming the laptop closed.

"Oh my god, Lara, can you at least knock?!" I shout, throwing a pillow at my roommate.

"Ew, gross!" she laughs, tossing the pillow right back at me. "For a virgin, you're such a perv, Maddie."

"I've got to be ready for them!" I whine, peeking out from the covers at her as she comes in. "There's no other way to do that!"

"Yeah, this is totally a test you can just study for," she jokes, rolling her eyes. "You're really going through with their offer, huh?"

I squirm, blushing. "Don't make fun of me..."

Lara rolls her eyes as she goes into the bathroom. "Two rich college boys, one preppy little virgin, and anything they want to do with you. Sounds like a guy's wet dream. What if it's a scam?"

I'd do it anyway, I think, ashamed of myself.

"They're offering to pay my tuition," I say softly. I've always been a shy, sweet girl. But I can't resist this.

"Just be careful, Maddie," she says. "You might get more than you can handle."

That's what I'm hoping for.

~

The door opens right after I knock, and I'm so nervous I could die.

The two guys who 'bought' me for the night don't live on campus. They're both sons of billionaires, and they live in a mansion way outside town. I'm worried I have the wrong address at first, but as soon as I see them open the door, I know I'm at the right place.

And my jaw drops.

"Brett? Mike?" I say, and I hug my coat tighter around me as the guys' expressions light up.

"Well well," Brett says, crossing his muscular arms, "if it isn't little Maddie."

I can't believe this. When I signed the contract

online, I didn't see the pictures of the guys, just their names.

I had no idea it would be the same Brett and Mike who tormented me during high school. They were a couple of aggressive jocks who got all the pussy in the world, and I was the shy little nerd they always teased. Both are towering over me, blonde, completely ripped, and looking gruffer and more mature than I remembered.

I hated them...but they were also the reason I had this stupid fantasy of getting taken by two guys. They joked about both of them taking me out on a date once, and the thought never left me, even though they were being mean.

"You've certainly changed, Maddie," Mike says, drinking me with his eyes. "Come on in, let's see you."

I blush furiously. I'm wearing nothing under my big fur coat and high heels, just like the contract said, but I feel so embarrassed I want to run away.

"What's the matter, Mads?" Brett teases, taking my coat and pulling me inside. I don't stop him. "Having second thoughts?"

"I didn't know it would be *you two*."

"So you'd do it with strangers?" Mike says as he closes the door behind me, trapping me in this massive, lavish manor. "That's not the Maddie I know."

"Wait, you still want this? With me?" I ask in disbelief.

"You didn't know we always liked you, Maddie?" Mike says, and I'm shocked when he comes up behind me and puts his hips against my ass. I feel his cock thick already, and I go redder than my hair. "We both did, we just didn't want to share back then."

"We're more open minded, now," Brett says, stepping forward and cupping my face in his big, rough hand. I'm getting wet already, and I hate myself for it, but this is a fantasy coming true. "Why'd you think the contract asked for a redhead just your height? But I never thought we'd land the *actual* Maddie."

It all made sense now, and there was no backing out. One night, anything they wanted, no condoms, and all my tuition would be paid off by the huge paycheck they were giving me.

"You can still leave," Brett says, running his thumb over my lower lip. "Says so in the contract. But as soon as this is off and little Maddie shows us what she's got," he says, bringing his hand to my coat, "you're all ours."

He says it in such a husky tone that my head swims. I bite my lip...and before I can give myself time for doubt, I shrug the coat off my body.

I'm on the short side, and I have pale skin with freckles on my shoulders. My breasts are round and firm, and I'm a little proud of my ass, which my long red hair almost touches. I can still smell my strawberry perfume. All in all, I think I look okay, but Brett is looming over me with a look on his face like he wants to tear into me right then.

Imagine my surprise when he does just that.

Brett steps forward and presses his lips to mine, and I suck in a sharp breath as he grabs my tits and squeezes. I'm ashamed to realize my nipples are already stiff and probably have been since I saw these two again.

He backs me up into Mike, who's like a stone wall, and I feel his thick cock on my naked butt.

What are you doing, Maddie?!

I'm living out my teenage fantasy, that's what.

"Someone's happy to see us," Brett says as he rubs his thumbs over my nipples in little circles. I can't hold back a groan as he does, because Mike's hands are holding my hips to his, and I feel his mouth on my neck, ravishing my soft skin.

"Has little Mads been thinking about this?" Mike whispers into my ear.

"I bet she studied for this," Brett says when he breaks away from my lips.

All I can do is whimper, I can't even defend myself against their incessant teasing. Suddenly, I feel like an awkward, gawky teenage nerd again, wishing the big jocks would pay attention to me.

All that time, I told myself it wouldn't be worth it.

But with Brett's hands fondling me and Mike's on my ass, I know my expectations are already blown out of the water.

Mike slips his hand around my hips, and I whimper when his finger touches my clit. He starts playing with it as if I was just another one of his conquests, as if it comes naturally to him. I squirm and writhe, but Brett has my breasts feeling electrified, and I'm utterly helpless in their hands.

"Hold up, the contract said she has to be a virgin," Mike says as he sticks his finger a little deeper into my wet pussy, discovering how ready I am for them. "Does that mean…?"

"Aww, Maddie was too shy to get a little action!" Brett mocks me as he takes a turn kissing my neck. I give a whimper of protest and try to squirm away, but they have such a hold on me that I'm totally theirs now.

"Waiting for us, Mads?" Mike growls into my ear, and while he moves his finger around my clit, he starts grinding into my ass. "Well you might like to know that no matter who we've dated all this time...we've just had you on our minds."

"God, you're so much hotter than I fantasized," Brett adds, giving my breasts a squeeze that makes me melt in Mike's arms. "You wanna take her upstairs, bro?" he asks Mike.

The way they talk about me, it's like I'm a toy to them. I shouldn't like this. I don't want to like this. But I feel my cunt getting wetter at the thought of being tossed around by them, and Mike's exploring my clit is only making it worse.

"Let's get her warmed up, first," Mike says.

"That's what I was thinking," Brett agrees, and he flicks my nipples with his thick fingers. I moan, but I get silenced by Brett's kiss. I feel his stubble scratch my face as his tongue explores my mouth, and I can't help but let him in.

He tastes like whiskey, and I smell manly cologne on him. I know he wants to push his hips against mine, but he's giving Mike room to finger me.

For his part, every time Mike's teeth graze my

neck, I feel like I'm already right on the edge of coming.

"This won't take long at all, will it?" Mike says with a chuckle. "I think Maddie has a crush on us."

"Here I thought we were getting the better end of the deal," Brett growls.

Brett's hands on my breasts is like nothing I could have imagined. Actually having a man give them attention is totally different than me playing with myself. He feels their weight, flicks my stiff nipples with his thumbs, and lets his fingers dance across them.

My breasts are smooth and full, but he makes them feel so much better just by touching them.

Mike is rubbing his fingers over my clit better than I've ever been able to rub myself. Between him and Brett at my breasts, I feel my body starting to revolt against me. Everything in my brain says not to let this happen, but I want it. I want it so badly, and I have for so long.

Waves of heat start to pulse from the sensitive nub between my legs, and I let out a long, low whine as I try to close my legs, but Mike's hands are strong, and his fingers are good at working their way inside me.

I start to push my hips up into his hand, and he

controls me with just that one arm. My lower abdomen starts to feel tense, and if Brett's tongue weren't halfway down my mouth, my jaw would fall open.

Memories are flooding back to me. I felt so jealous when I saw how they flirted with their girlfriends. I wanted them to be touching me like that.

And now, they are, and it's so much better than all the dreams I had about this.

"None of our girlfriends ever wanted this," Mike whispers. "It takes something special to act on it. You've wanted this, haven't you, Maddie?"

How the hell can they read me like an open book?

"You've been too quiet, Maddie," Mike goes on. "Let's hear you say it. The contract says anything we want. I want to hear you beg for us."

Brett pulls his lips away from my mouth, and he goes to my neck while Mike teases my clit. He's going just slow enough to keep me from cumming, and he knows it.

"Come on, Mads," he insists. "Beg for us. Tell us how much you want it."

"I…" I start, but I'm so dizzy from lust that I can't think straight. "I want…"

"Who do you want?"

"I want both of you," I moan in a pleading tone. "God, I've been thinking about this for so long! The contract was like a dream come true. All I want is for you two to fuck me so hard I can't breathe!"

Mike leans so close to my ear that I can feel his hot breath inside it.

"Good girl."

He hooks his fingers inside my pussy while his thumb brushes my clit, and I feel myself spill over the edge of cumming. I cum on his hand while I let out a long, deep sigh, and I thrash in their grip as the feeling shakes my whole body.

Mike's cock is hard on my ass, and his grip is so, so strong. Brett's hold on my tits and my neck means there's no escape--it's an overwhelming feeling on every one of my most sensitive spots.

When I finally stop cumming, Mike slides his fingers out of my pussy, and he brings my cum up to his mouth, where I hear him suck it off before he playfully pinches my cheek with clean fingers.

"Let's get you upstairs."

Brett steps back, and I melt into Mike's arms before he scoops me up bridal-style.

I'm a dizzy mess as he carries me up a huge set of wooden stairs, then down a hallway to a bedroom.

"This one's mine," Brett says proudly as he pushes

the door open. Inside is the biggest bed I've ever seen, so comfortable and firm-looking with satin sheets and natural moonlight filtering in from a window on the ceiling. It draws my eye so much I barely notice the rest of the gorgeous room.

Best of all, it smells like Brett's cologne and his natural musk.

Mike carries me to the bed and tosses me onto it, and I yelp as I bounce. He takes hold of my ankles and pulls me to the edge so he can pull my shoes off for me and toss them aside.

"We're a little impatient," Mike says with a wink as Brett starts to strip, but he stops halfway through pulling his shirt off.

"Hold up, Mike," he says with a wicked smile. "This is Maddie, after all. Let's make her work for this."

"I like how you think," Mike chuckles at me, and he nods at my legs. "Why don't you show us how much you like what you see?"

"Huh?" I ask, confused.

"Mike hasn't gotten a chance to see you in action," Brett says, and he makes a swirling motion with his fingers between his thighs. My eyes widen as I realize what he means.

"C'mon, Maddie," Mike growls. "Do it for me?"

I bite my lip. "I fucking hate you both so much," I whimper, but I find myself opening my legs wide for them.

I've never been so exposed for anyone in my life. I never thought my first time would be for these two.

My fingers touch my overstimulated clit, and I whimper as I feel electricity shoot up my body again. But the boys reward me for it.

Both of them strip their shirts off at the same time, and I swear, it's like a dream come true. Their muscles are perfect, with endless abs running down to a V that hints at how strong their crotches are. They kick their shoes off, then undo their pants and toss those to the side.

I start moving my fingers faster around my pussy, my big blue eyes flitting to each one as they strip for me. Soon, there's nothing left on either of them but their boxers, and I'm already feeling close to the edge.

"I've always wanted to have you in my room," Brett says as he approaches me, and I see the massive bulge sticking straight out from his boxers. "But this? This is better than any of the times I thought about you in the shower."

I let out a whimper at that thought, and I feel my

body tensing up, ready to come at any second already.

Then Brett drops his boxers.

His cock is long, thick, and ribbed with veins. His dark, bulging crown looks like it's desperate to be inside something.

Mike does the same, and his is just as unbelievable. I had no idea the two of them were like this, but I always hoped.

"Alright, good girl," Brett says teasingly as he gets on his knees and pushes my legs apart. "I've always wondered how you tasted."

Before I can react, he sticks his face to my cunt and lets out his tongue. I want to stop him, but I'm already so, so close to cumming that my body won't let me. The next second, I feel my high school bully's tongue run up my slit and lick up the honey I've been spilling on my fingers.

I toss my head back and lean on my elbows as heat crashes up my body. I'm right on the brink, and Brett's moaning as he works his tongue toward my clit only pushes me closer. His tongue is strong and huge, and it's so nimble that the tip plays with my clit in a way that makes me feel just as good as when Mike had me.

His tongue darts out over and over again, to the

point that I feel like a guitar string pulled so tight I'm about to snap.

Mike approaches, massaging his cock, and just the sight of him with Brett eating me out does it for me.

I squeeze Brett's head between my thighs and let out a long, high-pitched squeal as I come on Brett's face, dousing him in my honey, and he doesn't let up. His tongue keeps washing over me, pushing my lower lips aside and exploring the place that's been so private, so sacred to me all my life.

I'm these guys' toy now, and I'm loving every second of it.

"Damn, Maddie, you made a mess," Brett growls, and I swallow, ashamed of myself. Brett crawls up the bed to me, looming over me with a face covered in my own juices. "Let's see how you like it." He presses his lips to mine, wetting my face with my own cum, but that isn't what he meant.

He shoves his whole cock into me without warning.

I scream into his kiss, but he holds me with a grip so tight I doubt he can even feel me thrashing. Once he's down to the hilt in me, he breaks the kiss and sits up, scooting us back and picking up one of my legs to drape over his shoulder.

"Hey Mike, you got a good angle?"

"Almost," Mike says as he gets on the bed to my right, sizing me up.

"Got you covered, bro," Brett says, and he takes hold of my hair to tilt my head back and make me face Mike. My mouth is hanging open, and I feel like a bow pulled way back, between his cock and his grip. He has me paralyzed and helpless as Mike gets on the bed, his cock bobbing softly as he smiles.

"Perfect," Mike says, and my eyes widen as I realize what he's about to do. He reaches out and strokes my face gently, looking down at me with a lustful smile. "I always liked your lips, Maddie," he says. "Why don't you show me what you wanted to use them for?"

I know what he means, and when that realization hits me, I feel my pussy tighten and get wet all over again.

"I think she likes you, Mike," Brett says, grunting as I clench my pussy around him. I look up, and I see Mike's massive cock looming over me, and he's lowering it to my mouth.

"Let's make your dreams come true, Maddie," he growls.

I take his cock in my lips without a second thought.

The smell of his cock is musky and heady, and I close my eyes and moan as he slides it into my mouth. I feel its weight on my tongue, and I think it's heavier than I imagined, but he just keeps putting more and more of it in.

My mind goes to the girl who looked just like me in that porn I was watching. I try to channel her as much as I can, but there's just so much cock.

I keep taking it in until it hits the back of my throat. I feel my gag reflex trying to kick in, and tears spring to my eyes...

...but then Brett starts bucking into me.

Wave after wave of bliss washes through me as I feel his cock exploring my cunt just the way I always wanted. His strong hands grip my sensitive inner thighs and play with the soft skin while Mike runs his hand through my hair while the other hand goes to my stiff nipple and starts playing with it.

I signed up to be their toy for the night, but it feels like they're the ones paying to give me everything I've ever fantasized about.

My body is on fire. Every erogenous zone on me is lit up and over sensitive like never before. With Brett pumping into me, I feel the courage to keep my gag reflex down, and I power through the feeling of the bulging tip of Mike's cock in my mouth.

I'm going to get through it, for him.

Having a cock in me is better than I could have imagined. My roommate always raved about having a dildo, but I was too shy to buy one.

His thick girth makes every fraction of an inch inside me feel so loved, appreciated, and blissful. The groaning of the two guys over me makes me feel like I've never felt before. It's exciting and relaxing all at the same time.

I can already feel my body starting to get tight from Brett's thrusting, but I need to give Mike the attention he deserves. I have no idea how to give a blowjob, so I just start doing what feels natural.

I move my tongue up and down, and I'm rewarded by feeling Mike grip my hair and draw in a sharp breath. "Fuck, Maddie," he groans.

That gives me courage. I get a little bolder and start running the tip of my tongue from the base of his shaft as far to the tip as I can, over and over again, and I feel the cock throb and pulse inside me.

When I feel a bead of precum drop in the back of my throat, it's like a birthday present for all my hard work, and I feel a wave of happiness hit me.

Mike starts to help me out by moving his cock back and forth in my mouth. That just makes my head spin with ideas. I start darting my tongue to every part of his cock I can reach. When he almost pulls out entirely, I take the chance to lavish his crown with attention, and as he slides it back in, I make sure that every second he moves, he gets as much of my tongue's pressure as I can put on him.

Turns out, I'm pretty good at blowjobs, if Mike's moaning is anything to judge by.

But Brett is one giant, amazing distraction between my legs. He goes deeper and deeper, his crown grinding against every part of my insides that he can get to. I start shuddering as he finds ones that I like. He's so in tune with my body that he knows exactly how to give attention to the best parts of me.

It's almost like he's searching for something, but I don't know what.

Then, suddenly, it hits me.

I've always been studious, but sex ed was never my thing. I didn't even know what a clit was until college. I heard Lara talk about her g-spot, but I never asked what she meant. I only picked up that it was really, really good.

And the second Brett hits my g-spot with that thick, dark crown, god, *I know it.*

My whole body feels like a live wire, twitching and pulsing, and I moan sharply into Mike's cock just as I'm running my tongue up it.

That awakens something else in Mike, and suddenly, both the guys seem to turn their game up more than a few notches.

Brett starts pounding into me harder and faster, like a piston, hitting that g-spot over and over again with his thick crown. Mike starts ramming into me until he can feel the back of my throat, but my gag reflex just isn't there anymore.

In a moment of endless, sweet bliss, I feel just like that lucky girl in the video I was watching, getting pounded from both sides by two guys who are groaning, grunting, and panting, all because of me and my body.

"God, you're so fucking tight, Maddie," Brett groans.

"That's it, Maddie," Mike groans, "just a little more, come on, girl…!"

I feel my whole body winding up, and I feel a little bit afraid in the last few moments. I don't know how, but I can just feel that my body is about to do something bigger and harder than it ever has before.

The guys can feel it, too, and they lose all control.

Brett starts pounding into me with wild abandon, losing his rhythm. He's just rutting into me like a beast. Mike starts thrusting in my mouth so hard I think he mistook it for my cunt, but somehow, I handle it, lavishing his tongue with more stroking than I thought I was capable of.

"Yeah, yeah, that's it baby, oh fuck!" Brett groans, and for a split second, all three of us go silent as we all reach our peaks at the same time.

Then the hardest orgasm I've ever felt in my life hits me.

My whole body writhes as tension and relaxation spreads out from my pussy to every limb of my body. Touching myself pales in comparison to this. I am paralyzed, and then I feel a shot of seed fill my cunt at the same time that Mike releases in my mouth.

His cum is salty and delicious, and I moan as it pours over my tongue. I feel like I was releasing these guys' tension, tension that we've felt ever since we all met each other. Meanwhile, they're doing everything for me I've ever dreamed of and more.

My guys pump me full of cum on both ends, shot after shot entering me and filling me up. I can't get enough of it. Every time I feel them pulse in me, I want more. I clench my pussy and milk Brett for everything he has, and I bring my tongue to Mike's slit to tease out every last drop.

Mike finally pulls his cock from my mouth, and I

get to look it in the slit just before a final surge of white shoots out from it and hit me in the face.

I let out a blissful, delighted sigh as it dribbles down my face to my lips, and I lick it off before another spurt hits my breasts. I rub it into me as Brett empties the rest of himself into my cunt. I'm stuffed full, and I want more, so much more.

The guys are panting in ragged, tired breaths as I finish them off. I feel so, so theirs, and it's like swimming through a dream.

My heart flip-flops as I realize I forgot to take my birth control pill. But when I look up at Mike and Brett...it doesn't matter. I like it. And I want more.

When they finally pull their cocks out of me, I feel slightly less whole, and I reach for Mike's balls to stroke them affectionately. Mike grins and brings his manhood down to my mouth, and I lick it clean while batting my eyes up at him.

"I think she likes us, Mike," Brett says.

"I think I do too," I say, glancing at both the men. All three of us are glowing, and I've never felt more fulfilled in my entire life. "I don't suppose you're open to renewing the contract for another night?"

"How about another night *and* another morning?" Mike says, grinning down at me.

"I like that idea," I say. "Besides...it sounds like we have a lot of catching up to do."

"I agree," Brett says as he strokes my thigh, and it gives me a final shiver of delight. I look into his smiling eyes and feel nothing but warmth. "Maddie, I think this is the start of a very good relationship."

~

Six months later, Mike lifts his face from my soaked pussy as I feel another orgasm wash over me.

It's getting harder to see him over my pregnant belly every time he lifts his face, but the look of pure joy in his smile never gets old.

As he does, I feel Brett's hands wiping his cum off my breasts while peppering my face in kisses.

"I swear to god, you just get hotter with every month," Brett says as he runs his hand over my swollen stomach. I was nervous about being pregnant around my two favorite guys, but they both know it's their baby in there, and ever since that first night we took the plunge to be together, we've been inseparable.

"It feels like you two get more enthusiastic every week," I say as Mike rubs my thighs while Brett massages my shoulders. "If this is how you are, I might just have to stay pregnant after this one."

"That won't be a problem," Brett whispers into my ear. "Because we're going to get you knocked up with our babies again and again and again, as long as you want."

I turned to kiss Brett on the lips, flashing my sparkling engagement rings with a playful smile.

"Careful what you wish for, Brett," I say. "Forever is a long time."

CATERING TO HER

"You ou look a little lonely, why don't you join us in here?"

I stop walking and turn my head ever so slightly to look back toward the steaming hot tub, not sure whether that thick, husky voice is talking to me or not. When my eyes fall on the speaker, though, I can't believe my eyes.

"Yeah, blondie, he's talking to you," says the second man with a cocky smile.

Jack Marlowe and Aiden Scott, two of the hottest guys in Hollywood, are soaking in the bubbling, steaming water, and if I didn't know better, I'd think both of them were absolutely devouring me with their eyes.

I'm just one of the catering girls. My blonde hair is on the curly side and cut well above my shoulders, and I have a curvy frame that suits my modest button-down shirt and skimpy skirt and heels well. The cherry-red lipstick and subtle rose perfume I'm wearing was probably more than was necessary, but I like a little extra effort in my looks. Still, I don't think I'm Hollywood material.

When I got the call this morning that I was supposed to cater for one of those exclusive Hollywood house parties you only hear about in the tabloids, I couldn't believe it. Having broken up my good-for-nothing boyfriend who didn't even bother to pop my cherry last week, I was in the mood for something new and exciting, and this got my heart racing.

When I slipped some of the most expensive, frilly, lacy lingerie on under my professional catering outfit, I assumed it would just be something to give me a boost of confidence.

My risque underwear would be my little secret.

I never expected to turn heads at the party, much less the heads of the two guys I'd spent more than a little time thinking about in my private time in the bathtub.

"Usually," Aiden says, turning to lean his bare arms against the concrete, "when Jack Marlowe says 'come', girls listen."

"Maybe she's shy, Aiden," Jack says. "Or just tired. We've been watching her all night, we know how hard she's been working."

My heart flutters. Just how much have they been watching me?

"Alright, then come bring some of those drinks over to us," Aiden says. He hooks his finger and beckons me with a smile that makes my heart melt.

I've been a fan of their movies since as long as I can remember. Both these guys are almost ten years older than me, but they look better than anyone my age that I've ever met.

Jack has short black hair and the perfect amount of scruff on his face, and his piercing blue eyes are so clear and bright that I feel like they can see right through my clothes.

And I kind of like that idea.

Aiden is the perfect foil to him. He has shaggy blonde hair that makes him look like a surfer, and his face is clean shaven to show off his perfectly tanned skin and deep green eyes.

If you believed the tabloids, Jack was the gruff

one with a heart of gold, while Aiden was the forward and fiery one. The idea of finding out whether either is true sends a ripple of excitement up my back.

"What can I get you gentlemen?" I ask in my best server's tone as I approach them slowly. My heart beats faster as I realize I'm swaying my hips on my way over to them, and both of them grin at the sight.

"Think I'd like a tall drink of *you*," Aiden says, and Jack rolls his eyes.

"Couple glasses of champagne, but I want you to join us," Jack says.

His tone makes it clear that isn't a suggestion. It is a kind but firm order. My cheeks go red, and I can't help but smile.

"I might get in trouble for drinking on the job," I say.

"Are you even legal to drink?" Aiden purr as I approach. As I step close enough to look right down at them, I realize he's looking up my legs with hungry eyes.

"Would they let me serve if I wasn't?"

Jack grins at Aiden. "She's got bite. I like her."

"I do too," Aiden muses. "Legs that go on for days, blonde Marilyn Monroe hair, ruby-red lips, and eyelashes that could kill a man? You're not getting paid enough for this, young lady."

"What do you think of the party?" Jack asks, a little sincerity in his voice. I feel my heart racing, and I just blurt out the first thing that comes to mind on pure impulse.

"I think I like you two calling me 'young lady.'" The words couldn't have been mine. I can't believe it!

I've always been a girl who knows what she likes. I'm ashamed to admit it, but my laptop's search history is crammed with so much porn that you'd think I make the stuff.

Specifically, I spend almost every night looking for videos about two guys having one girl to themselves.

It's always interested me. I don't know what it is about that combo, but the thought of two men grabbing me everywhere my ex was too much of a wimp to go, two husky voices whispering into my ear...just the thought gets me worked up.

And right now, I'm standing over a couple of guys who don't even know they're hitting on my deepest, darkest secret.

Aiden's face lights up, and Jack sits back in the tub and strokes his scruffy chin with a wolfish smile.

"I'll call you a few more things if you serve us those drinks," Aiden growls.

I can't believe I'm doing this.

I'm going to get so fired if I indulge them too much. My boss is strict about this kind of thing. The last thing the company wants is its girls getting tossed around by the celebrities they're supposed to be working for.

But these two...

I take a couple of glasses between my hands and bend over, serving one glass to Aiden while making sure to give Jack a good, long look at my ass. I hear a murmur of approval from him, and I feel my cheeks go even redder as Aiden's hand brushes mine while he takes both glasses for himself.

When he winks, it feels like an arrow shooting me through the heart, and I love it.

I reward him by turning and giving him a turn looking at me as I serve Jack, whose smoky eyes hold me entranced for a few moments while he takes just the one glass.

"You've got one more glass on that tray," Jack says. "Sit."

Almost everyone is gone from the party by now. This is Jack's house, and everyone knows Aiden has been his best friend for years. They're in their action movies together all the time.

I hesitate for a second. If I do this and someone finds out about it, I'm definitely fired.

Then I remember my ex. A month ago, I thought we were going to get married. Life changes way too fast to worry.

I lift my foot and slip off one of my shoes, then the other, and Aiden's grin widens as I step into the hot water and feel it hug my legs. I sit down and set my tray aside to reach for the drink, but Jack holds up a hand.

"Oh no, you're *much* too overdressed. Come over here."

My mouth falls open. I look into the water, and I think his words over.

I know exactly where he's going with this. But do I really want to throw this job away for this?

I know the answer before I'm done asking myself.

Swallowing, I slip into the bubbling water and sink up to my waist. My skirt floats up, and Aiden gives a cheer as I wade across the water to get to Jack, who opens his wide arms to receive me. Before I know it, he's sitting me down on his thick, strong leg in the hot tub, and his arms wrap around my form to start unbuttoning my shirt.

"I like this kind of catering," he says, and he scoots my ass a little closer to his lap. I gasp as I feel his thick cock on my ass, and I realize he's hard as a rock.

"Don't be so surprised," he purrs into my ear as he finishes unbuttoning my shirt. "Aiden and I noticed you the second your pretty ass walked through the door. I think you could use a break."

"She's wearing lingerie under the outfit," Aiden says, nodding to my exposed chest. "She came prepared!"

"Well well, you're full of surprises," Jack says, looking over my shoulder. "What's your name, sweetheart?"

"Sophie," I say, barely above a whisper.

"Sophie," Jack says. The way he says my name sends a shiver up my back. "Sophie, we like you."

"I think I like you too," I say, and again, I'm amazed the words are coming from my lips.

"Is that why you wore all this nice lace for us?" Aiden asks, and I'm surprised when Jack moves me to sit beside him, and Aiden swoops in to my other side, sandwiching me between the two impossibly gorgeous male bodies.

"I think so," I say, and I nervously twirl my light blonde hair around a finger, batting my eyes at Aiden.

"Just 'think' so?" Aiden asks, and he wraps an arm around my waist under the water, and I feel his hand searching up my thigh. "Now that doesn't sound like the confident girl who just took the plunge to play with the big boys."

His fingers go up under my skirt and trace around my panties. He touches my pussy through the fabric, and I gasp and shiver.

I should be getting up and running away. I should be saying no. I should be responsible.

"Yes, sir," I purr instead, wiggling my hips up against Aiden and smiling coyly. "I've been under a lot of stress lately, and…"

"And you could use a little attention," Jack says, leaning in close to me. My eyes are lidded, and I don't look directly at him, which is why I'm surprised when I feel his large, strong hand on my left breast suddenly. He gives it a squeeze, and I suck in a sharp breath.

"Jack and I are good at giving girls like you attention," Aiden says, "but I can tell you're something special."

"I need a lot of attention," I say cautiously,

looking at both of them, and they look even hungrier than ever at those words.

"Good," Jack growls. "Aiden and I have wanted to share for a long time."

The words send a shiver up my spine, and I visibly writhe in delight at their touch.

"I was wrong, Jack," Aiden says with wide eyes. "I like this one a *lot*."

Jack rips my shirt off my shoulders and tosses it aside. Aiden pulls my skirt down, and I wiggle my hips until he can get it off my legs and let it float away uselessly.

"Damn, I like what I see," Aiden says, as he runs his hands up and down my legs and drinks in the sight of my lingerie. It's so rare to find guys who really appreciate good lace, and the fact that these two seem to like it makes me feel excited and proud all at once.

"Do you want a closer look?" I offer, pushing my hips up at him subtly, and he squeezes my hips in return.

"I want more than a look," he says.

He pulls my panties down to my knees under the water, making me feel almost trapped between that and Jack's hold on my arms.

Before I can react, Jack puts his mouth on my neck and kisses me.

My whole body lights up with desire. His scruff tickles my neck while his teeth graze my skin. My cunt is heating up and getting wetter, and I want nothing more than something big and thick to stuff between my thighs.

Then I feel Aiden lift up my hips and I watch as that thick shock of blonde hair goes underwater.

He goes between my thighs.

The next second, I let out a loud gasp as Aiden's tongue touches my pussy. It's a quick lick at first, just testing me. Then comes a second, braver lick. His hands squeeze my hips in approval, and I know deep down that he likes the taste of me. I just know it.

I knew tonight would be wild, but I never thought I'd be sandwiched between two of the hottest bodies in Hollywood.

Aiden's tongue starts darting out again and again, getting a little more of my pussy and its wetness each time, and while he does, I realize Jack has unhooked by bra. I feel it start to slip down my arms as he kisses me.

"I can smell your cologne," I whisper. Why did I

say that? What a stupid thing to say! But I feel Jack's mouth curl into a grin as he kisses me.

"I can smell your perfume," he says. "It's nice. I could get you something even nicer. You have good taste already."

His hands slip over my breasts, and he squeezes them. His grip is full of desire, and I push my chest up into him to give him more of me. I want him to take every little bit of me.

"Take all you want," I urge him.

"Oh, I will," he says, and I gasp as Aiden's tongue touches my clit. Having found it, he gets more aggressive, holding me closer to him and pressing his lips to my pussy and licking my clit over and over again. "But you can say 'stop' any time you want. Condom?"

"No," I breathed, shaking my head. "I want you both...bare."

He strokes my nipples with his thumbs, and I feel them getting stiffer. I still can't believe this is happening. He presses his chest into me, and I feel every one of his rock-hard abs against my soft body.

"How long can he hold his breath?" I ask Jack, nodding down to Aiden.

"A long time," Jack growls, and he flicks my nipples before he sliences me with a deep kiss on my lips. I feel him groan into my mouth, and his thick tongue dives in to explore me.

I let him, and at the same time, I feel Aiden's tongue exploring my lower lips. He seems to find his way around wonderfully, prodding and stroking wherever he wants, but every few seconds, he gives my clit the attention it so badly needs.

I start to feel tight in my abdomen already, and after a few more seconds of the sensation, Aiden brings his head above the water for breath.

He runs his hand through his wet, golden hair and smiles at me wolfishly, and my heart does a somersault as I watch those impeccable muscles on his arms and chest work together. He has a tattoo on his right pec, and I reach out to run my hands over his chest.

He takes the invitation and leans in to bring his mouth to my breasts.

He holds my hips and takes my left nipple between his teeth, and he slowly moves his teeth back and forth, gently toying with the swollen, sensitive bud. While he kisses my breasts, Jack kisses my mouth, and I feel his hand slip between Aiden's to hook a finger inside my cunt.

I moan into his mouth as I try to clench my legs, but he's too good at finding my clit. With two fingers, he starts to rub me in a little circle that sends ripples of heat up my body. I can feel both of them on every part of my body, and I'm reveling in it. I feel so free, so uninhibited, and I'm all for them while they're all for me.

Jack gets me closer and closer to the edge, and I start pushing my hips up into him while Aiden lavishes my breasts with attention. My breasts are full and heavy, and the fact that they're getting these guys so excited drives me wild.

My biggest fantasy is getting fulfilled, and the guys doing it are more into it than I ever thought they could be.

I start letting out little moans in a steady rhythm as I get closer and closer to the edge. But just when I feel like Jack is going to take me there, Aiden takes his lips from my breasts and chuckles.

"Oh no you don't," he growls, "I'm finishing what I started."

He dives back underwater, and Jack takes his fingers away to put both hands on my breasts.

"He always was the jealous one," Jack chuckles, and I start to reply when I feel Aiden's tongue in full force on my clit.

I squeal as I feel a shot of heat up my body, and it feels like electricity is welling up and spreading out from that swollen, sensitive nub. I don't know how he can do it underwater like that, but his tongue is relentless. Every time he licks deeper into me, he gets more of a taste of me, and he's drinking it all in.

His tongue darts in and out, over and over again, and I reach down to his hair to grab fistfuls of it as I get so close to the edge that I could scream.

Jack lets his teeth nip at my neck and squeeze my breasts hard, and at the same time, I feel my pleasure explode through my body. I let out a long, satisfied gasp as I come, and I feel my wetness spread out in the hot water under me, all over Aiden.

He doesn't let up when I come, but he licks me through to the end as I writhe in bliss against Jack's chest. He gives a deep, gravelly chuckle as I cum, and when it's finally over, Aiden comes up for breath and grins at my face.

"That's what I like to see," he says, taking my chin in his hand and stroking my lip with his thumb.

"Don't worry," Jack tells me. "We're not nearly done with you yet." His blue eyes flit up to Aiden. "Hold her for me."

"Come get a turn on my lap, honey," Aiden says, and he takes me and pulls me into position. As I move, Jack reaches down and pulls my panties the rest of the way off and tosses them out of the water.

Then he pulls his trunks off.

He stands up in the water, and my eyes go wide at the same time that Aiden pulls me into his lap. I yelp as I feel Aiden's naked cock on my ass, and he sits me down to press my soft ass against it while Jack approaches me.

Jack's cock looks every bit as big as Aiden's feels.

"Fuck, you two are huge," I breathe.

"Size doesn't matter, love," Aiden growls.

"It's what you do with it," Jack agrees, and he pushes my thighs aside and looks down at the distorted view of my pussy under the bubbling water. He sees the nervousness and anticipation in my face, and he smiles. "This is your first rodeo, isn't it, sweetheart?"

I nod reluctantly, and I feel Aiden's cock pulse with desire.

"Of course it is," Aiden growls. "But don't you worry, Sophie, we'll take care of you."

"I think you're a natural," Jack says.

"One way to find out," I whisper, and I yelp as Aiden pinches my nipples between his fingers and Jack grips my thighs.

"You're right about that," Jack growls.

He impales me against Aiden.

I let out a shout that Aiden covers with his big,

strong hand. The feeling is so sudden and surprising that I can't believe it, and I feel a twinge of pain, but it gets smothered in so, so much pleasure that I feel like I'm floating through a dream.

So many of my friends had their first times in the usual ways--awkward experimenting with a friend or some one-off relationship in high school. And that was fine for plenty of them.

But this? This is better than anything I could have imagined.

Jack is so thick that I feel like he won't fit inside me, but he manages to stuff his whole girth into me. At least, I think he does . I look down, and two things happen.

First, the sight of his thick shaft sticking out of me brings me so close to the edge that I realize I'm probably only a few thrusts away from cumming again. Second, I realize that his shaft is only halfway in my pussy.

"Fuck," I whimper, and the two guys laugh.

"Don't worry," Jack whispers, "I've got you."

Something about that gruff, almost fatherly voice sends a warm shiver up my body, and I want to give everything I have to these two.

From behind, Aiden is fondling my breasts while he grinds his thick cock against my ass. I've always been proud of my round, full ass and generous hips. But Aiden is more than proud of it. He's reveling in it as if it's a gift from heaven.

I hear him groan each time he thrusts up and squeezes my asscheeks around his shaft. I want to get him off with just my ass, but the idea of him taking a turn inside me thrills me too much.

"God, you're so fucking tight," Jack groans as he starts to thrust into me. He's gentle at first, rocking back and forth, and even then, I can feel his whole girth sliding in and out of me, every detail of it so thick and taut inside me. He goes a little deeper, and I feel his bulging crown work its way into me, probing for my most sensitive spots.

And he finds them.

He starts getting a steady rhythm up, and I let my head roll back onto Aiden's shoulder as I feel myself getting tenser and tenser. My toes curl, and my mouth hangs open as he fucks me deep.

I'm so wet and slick that it feels like he's cutting through butter in me. His hips are like an unstoppable piston, and his arms hold my hips so firmly that I feel like I'm just a toy for him to play with. And nothing has ever felt sweeter.

He kisses me on the mouth while Aiden kisses my neck, and I feel a bead of precum pulse into my wet cunt. I lift my head to look at Jack's rippling muscles, countless abs running down to his crotch, and I look down to watch his throbbing shaft pumping in and out of my cunt over and over.

The sight of that and the reality of my situation pushes me over the edge again.

I let out a scream that Aiden doesn't stop this time, and I feel my cunt pulse with release as warmth spreads out and shakes my whole body. As I come, Jack doesn't let up, just like Aiden didn't let up.

Only this time, Jack is letting himself spiral to his own release.

I'm about to have Jack Marlowe's cum fill me up.

The thought gets me close to coming again, riding off the coattails of the last one, and Jack loses his rhythm. He starts rutting into me furiously, gritting his teeth and pounding into me so fiercely that I worry he's going to break me, but he's so gentle yet so animalistic.

Finally, he clenches his eyes, and he lets out a ragged groan as I feel a shot of hot seed burst into my pussy.

Jack plasters his sticky seed all over my insides, shot after shot of the hot cum exploding into my needy lips as Jack lets out that moan of utter, complete release.

I feel his balls tightening with each shot of cum he pumps into me, and finally, it comes to an end, with Jack breathing heavily on top of me, just as a third, smaller orgasm ripples through my body.

Halfway through that orgasm, Jack pulls out of me, and I see him nod to Aiden with a grin on his face.

Jack's seed floats out into the water, and Aiden lifts me up.

"Oh fuck!" I whimper as I realize what's about to happen.

Aiden lowers me onto his cock from behind.

"Ohhhhh, god!" I cry out, and Aiden's cock pulses and throbs with triumph as it slides right into me.

This new angle is unbelievable. Jack was good, but Aiden is good in a completely different way. I can't compare the two--they're like fire and ice in all the best ways.

Aiden's cock feels different from Jack's, but it's just as thick and strong, and his bulging crown grinds up against the front of my pussy to hit new parts of me like a mirror image of Jack's.

I knew two guys would be good.

But this?

This couldn't be more validating and fulfilling.

Aiden bounces me on his cock like a toy, using both his hips and his arms to bring me up and down over and over again, and he grinds against my g-spot. It sends white-hot energy shooting through my body, and I feel another orgasm crash through me unexpectedly.

They come hard and fast now, or maybe it's all part of one long orgasm that just melds together. I can't even tell anymore. All I know is that I want more of it.

While Aiden bounces me on his cock, it's Jack's turn to have me from behind. His hands hold my breasts and press my back into his muscular torso. His still-stiff cock is between my asscheeks, pointing up. As Aiden's bouncing massages his cock with my ass, a final spurt of seed shoots out from his cock and tickles my back.

Even though he already came, Jack is panting into my ear, and it's so hot that I can't even tell the two men apart. They're a machine that works in perfect harmony.

And it's all for me.

"Cum one more time for me, blondie," Aiden growls while Jack flicks my nipples.

"Get me there," I beg him, "just a little further…!"

Those words are like magic on Aiden. He starts bucking up into me harder and faster than ever before. Each time I slide down his ribbed cock, I hit the base, and I realize he's all the way in me, throbbing with each motion. The soft underside of his cock massages my pussy while the tip sends me to new heights, and just when I think it can't get any better, I feel something stronger than ever welling up in me.

A full-body orgasm hits me at the same time that Aiden releases inside me, and I dig my nails into his thighs as I come, and we groan together while Jack electrifies my nipples with his rough, aggressive touch and his kisses on my neck.

Shot after shot fills me up, mixing with my honey and stuffing me more than I thought I was capable of. I don't know how long it lasts--I lose track of time.

But after what feels like a full minute, I realize it's over.

Aiden massages me with his cock as I come down from the high he gave me, and Jack's kisses get more gentle.

"Fuck, Sophie," Aiden growls. "You're in the wrong business."

"What business would you suggest I be in?" I

giggle at him while Jack reaches over to my forgotten serving tray. He picks up the glass of champagne and brings it to my lips to let me drink from his glass.

The champagne tastes sweeter than I remember. Between these two guys, everything would.

"The business of being ours," Jack says.

I nearly choke on the champagne. "W-what?"

"You heard him," Aiden says. I'm still on his cock, and it's still stiff in me. "I want more of this, Sophie, and so does Jack."

"So much more," Jack growls. "Aiden and I live together. Don't you think that would beat catering? Lounge around in our manor all day and get taken by the two of us every night."

I don't even know how to respond.

"You're...kind of describing a dream come true," I breathe, almost laughing.

Jack leans in and kisses me on the neck and whispers into my ear. "That's exactly what I was going to say."

I did get fired from my catering job. It

turned out that someone had spotted me and reported me to my boss.

I couldn't care less.

Four months later, I was bouncing on Aiden's dick again, but this time, I was in their four-poster bed, and I had a bump in my belly showing.

It was their baby, and they knew it.

Jack was kissing me on the lips while Aiden's hands groped my breasts, and our groans were filling the massive master bedroom.

Every day was like this, just like they promised. When they weren't on movie sets raking in more billions of dollars, I was lounging in the manor buying more outfits and lingerie and fancy foods than I could ever know what to do with. And when they did get home, exploring their bodies was a new and exciting adventure each day.

"Fuck, I love you, Sophie," Jack groaned.

"We both love you," Aiden growled into my ear. The two liked to pretend to fight over me, but I knew they both loved me equally, and they were the best of friends for it. I was their common love, and it worked. It didn't matter whether anyone understood.

It was working, and better yet, we had a marriage

officiator who was going to marry me to both of them.

Life was good.

And with their baby on the way and endless, blissful nights on the horizon...it looked like life was just getting started.

EXHIBITIONIST FOR HER

I can't believe she talked me into this.

My lips curve into the best smile I can muster in the mirror, and I push my breasts up in the skimpy lingerie that doesn't do anything to hide my body. There's glitter on my chest and arms, and the room is thick with the scent of flowery perfume. My brown hair is styled into big curls that spill over my shoulder, and my long eyelashes couldn't be better.

But I'm still more nervous than I was when I graduated.

My outfit for the night is classy, at least, compared to what I was expecting. I'm wearing a white thong around my hips, but I don't have a bra. Instead, I have a sheer white negligee with a sash

CANDY QUINN

tied around my stomach that holds it all together. My nipples are obvious underneath it, and it's chilly enough in the changing room that they're stiff.

"Ready for your debut?" my friend Tiffany asks as she walks up behind me, beaming at my outfit. "Oh my god, you look kinky."

"Shut up!" I whine.

"Own it, girl!" she insists, patting me on the ass. She's wearing frilly pink and black panties with matching nipple covers and a fluffy pink boa around her shoulders. She looks a little more sultry than me, I think--at least, I want to think so.

I've always been the shy one, at work and in school and in my social life.

So, how did Tiffany convince me to take a job at this high-end sex club?

Money, duh.

I lived my whole life never partying, never going out to drink, and never even bothering with guys. I was pretty awkward in high school, after all.

But I'm an adult now. I just never expected my adult life to be quite like this.

"Alright, it's showtime," Tiffany says. "Come on, let's go!"

Tiffany grabs my hand and pulls me out the door

SHARING HER

to the club floor, and I feel my anxiety boil up inside me immediately.

The pink lights in the club are dim, casting long, seductive shadows and only hinting at everything that's going on around the place. The music is soft and ambient, and I feel its pulse in my every breath.

This is a public sex club.

And the music is doing nothing to hide the sounds of it.

As Tiffany and I walk through the club, I look to my right, and my eyes widen.

A man in a suit is reclining in a chair, and there's a girl riding him. When she brings her hips up, I catch a glimpse of his cock in the pink light. It's glistening with her honey, and the way they're both moaning makes me think they're both into it.

That could be me.

The thought comes unbidden to me. I blush. I don't normally have those thoughts, but I keep glancing back at the two as Tiffany leads me along.

We pass a long, luxurious red couch where a man in a mask is bent over a girl my age, one of her legs draped around his shoulder while he pumps into her, and to their right is a third girl reclining on the couch and touching herself while she watches the two.

My cheeks get even redder. I'm surprised all these people seem really *into* this, but at the same time, I can't tear my eyes away from each group of people we pass.

"Hey hey, in a hurry?" a male voice calls from nearby, and we both turn our heads. There's a large man with a big beard sitting alone in a booth with a drink, and he hooks a finger to beckon Tiffany. "Yeah, you--pink boa."

Tiffany looks at me with a bright smile. "Sorry, Amanda, I gotta take this one."

"W-wait, don't leave me alone!" I try to say, but Tiff is already on her way to her man. My jaw drops as I watch her descend into his hands, and immediately, he sticks his fingers into her panties and starts going to work on her clit.

I put a hand to my mouth in shock. This is my friend...but even I can't take my eyes away for a few seconds. Why am I so fascinated by all this?

I finally turn and hurry away. This was a mistake. I need to get out of here. And yet...

My license might say that I'm too young to drink, but I start making my way to the bar, wondering if the bartender would give me a pass. But I don't make it halfway there before something catches my attention and holds it paralyzed.

Across the room on an elevated platform is a corner booth. It's cozy, and there are lights behind the seats that give it a certain allure, but it's still almost as exposed as the rest of the seating. There are two dark figures sitting there. I can't make out their features, but they both have tall, striking frames and are wearing crisp button-down shirts rolled up to the sleeves.

And they're looking right at me.

I try to look behind me to see if they're eyeing someone different, but when I look back, they're chuckling at my naivety. I'm paralyzed. If I went up to them and they don't want me, I'd die of embarrassment.

One of them raises his hand and gestures for me to come, just like Tiffany's guy did, and I feel my cheeks burning. But as if entranced by a spell, I feel my feet moving toward them, one step after the other.

Am I really doing this?

I walk up the steps slowly, and I realize I'm unconsciously swaying my hips. They seem to like that, and I feel butterflies in my stomach. The men have to be at least ten years older than me, and the idea that they like what they see is both scary and exciting.

But then, I get close enough to see their faces.

I gasp.

They're familiar faces.

It's Michael Pierce and David O'Connor...the two owners of the multi-billion dollar business my father works at. He's been their personal assistant for as long as I've been around.

And now, they're devouring me with their eyes.

"Well well, look at the last face I expected to see at this place," Michael says in a very different voice than I remember. "Does your daddy know you're here, Amanda?"

A shiver goes up my back. The mood of the club was already putting me into a strange, unfamiliar headspace, but hearing Michael's voice talking to me like that does something to me.

"I never would have guessed," David says, leaning forward. "Here I thought you were just a cute little bookworm."

He remembers that about me? I've been around these men plenty of times in my life, but I never thought for a second that they were looking at me like...this.

"Um, hi," I squeak, barely above a whisper, and I wave my hand a little, completely at a loss for what to do. I feel embarrassed when the men chuckle at that.

"I think she's new at this, David," Michael says in a smooth tone.

"She doesn't know how good at it she is," David agrees. "Come over here, sweetheart. Want to make some good tips?"

"Wait, wh-what?" I say, my eyes going wide. I look down at my chest and remember that I'm almost totally exposed--my dad's friends can see my nipples! I cover myself and bite my lip. "Please don't tell Dad!"

The men laugh a little more at that, but one of them reaches out for my hand. "Don't you worry, hon, we won't tell anyone if you come get comfortable."

I look between the two of them. How could I be so naive? Seeing them here was so surprising that I just forgot what they're here for and what they must have called me over for.

"D-do you mean…?"

"That's right," Michael says, and he points down at his lap. "Come on, Amanda. I remember how you used to look at me."

My face goes red, even as I find myself walking

toward him. I used to have a huge crush on them both, of course, but who didn't at that age?

Both men were well over six feet tall, and both of them worked out to perfection. I could always tell by the way their suits hung on their shoulders, but with their forearms exposed, it was plain as day. They were ripped. Michael's green eyes and David's blue ones were both piercing, and just one glance from them could get my body turned on.

"You do?" I ask, and he spreads his legs for me to take a seat on his lap. I hesitate for a second, but then, a new kind of courage stirs up in me. It's a courage I didn't know was in me, but seeing Michael so ready for me like he is brings it out.

Our eyes lock for a few more seconds before I slowly turn around and give the men a good look at my ass. Michael reaches up and puts his big, rough hand on my asscheek and squeezes it. Energy runs up my body, and I feel more excited than ever. He gropes me as I lower my butt to his lap, and from this angle, I can see most of the club before me.

Anyone who turned to look at us could see us if they wanted to.

I swallow and take a seat.

Immediately, I yelp at what I feel under me. Michael's thighs are toned and hard, but it's not the only thing that's hard down there. His manhood is practically bursting from his pants, and I feel the hard, long shaft pressing against my ass and my pussy through the thin fabric separating us.

"Good girl," Michael says. He puts his hands on my hips and squeezes me gently. "I've always liked you, Amanda. You're so good at listening to orders."

This is going against everything I know. I shouldn't like this. I feel shame in every part of my body. But in the darkness of the club, there's something exciting about just letting loose. It's not like I haven't had fantasies about this kind of thing.

And the fact that there are two of them makes it even better.

"I've always thought you were...nice," I say in a weak voice, and I feel a chuckle in Michael's chest. I'm not good at flirting.

"That's where you're wrong," Michael says, and to my surprise, he slips one of his hands around my waist and teases at the waistline of my panties. "David over there has always thought you have nice legs, you know. Why don't you show him?"

David is sitting at an angle next to Michael, and a grin is spreading across his face. I swallow and nod my head softly. I lift my legs up one by one, setting them on David's lap and leaving me sprawled across the two older men.

David puts one hand on my ankle and lets his other hand glide across my smooth legs, admiring them. "Damn," he murmurs. "Better than I ever imagined. Your father should be proud of you, Amanda."

"You thought of them?" I can't help but say. My heart is fluttering in my chest. I didn't know I had these buttons in me, but they're pressing every one of them.

David slips off one of my heels, then the other, letting them clatter to the ground. "We both have," he says in a low, husky tone. "Those long nights at the office give us a lot of imagination space."

"And you're a lot of fuel for that," Michael says, running his hands up my body. He pulls the sash open and lets my sheer covering fall loose around my arms. I shiver as his hands work up my stomach, so very close to my breasts. "All those times your dad brought you to work gave us some ideas. Of course, we never thought we'd get to act on them."

"...but if you're willing," David says, massaging my calves sensuously, "we could act out a few. And when we say good tips, you should know that you'd be getting a *lot* more than you usually get here."

I swallow nervously. "You'd be my...my first."

Michael's cock pulses under me, and I hear him suck in a sharp breath right by my ear. It makes me blush, and I feel myself getting warmer between my legs as my heart picks up. Did the idea of my virginity really excite them that much?

"Let me put it this way, then," David says. "College? You won't have to worry about debts, no matter where you went. Any car you want. Any place you could want to live. Downtown apartment in Boston? That's chump change."

"We want to spoil you, Amanda," Michael says, bringing his fingers dangerously close to my breasts. I want him to go just a little further so bad, but he's barely holding back. "The way we've always wanted to you while you pranced around the office, just out of our reach. All you have to do is say yes."

I put my small hand on his big, manly one. Every rational thought in me tells me to push it away and walk out now.

Instead, I slide his hand up to my breast, and he squeezes it with a firmness that sends fire through my whole body.

"Yes," I whisper.

David reaches past my legs and takes hold of my panties. He starts sliding them down my leg, kissing my thigh as he goes, and before he even gets them to my knees, Michael puts his fingers between my legs.

There's no more teasing, no more playfulness. Something changes about the men I'm sitting on. Something primal has awakened in them, and my young body is theirs for the taking.

I gasp as Michael touches my clit, and he starts rubbing it in little circles that send warmth through my whole body. I'm soaking wet down there, and I didn't realize it until he touched me.

"Fuck, Amanda," he groans into my ear while he plays with my nipple with his free hand, flicking and pinching it. "You never lost that crush on us, did you?"

"No, sir," I whimper as he touches me. It's true, and my words make his mighty cock throb under me. I try to rub my ass down into him to make it better for him. "Never."

David takes my panties off, and he brings the crotch of the fabric to his nose and breathes in deeply. Something his deep, husky groan gets me even more excited, and my eyes widen as I watch him take his belt off and unbutton his pants.

His cock springs out, and it's nearly enough to make me cum on its own, thanks to Michael's attention to my pussy.

It's long and thick, ribbed with veins and topped with a dark, bulging crown that looks like it could burst at any second. The heavy balls under the towering shaft promise even more of a release.

I whimper at the sight while Michael massages my pussy, and I feel myself getting closer and closer to release already. I can't believe it's taking so little time! I feel embarrassed and exposed, but fuck, it feels so good.

"You like that, don't you, Amanda?" Michael whispers in my ear, his eyes down on my exposed breasts. "It's okay to like it. Just wait 'till you see mine."

That makes me suck in a shuddering gasp, and I feel my body surging toward the edge of orgasm. Michael keeps rubbing my clit faster, and his hand seems unable to get tired. I feel tension start to well up in my lower abdomen, and it only gets more intense with each passing second.

Michael covers my mouth just in time to stop me from screaming out as my first orgasm from a man crashes through my body. Tension spreads out to my every limb and releases like soft bursts of burning heat, and I feel my pussy dousing Michael's hand.

"Good girl," he coos softly, "good girl, that's it."

I should hate the way he's talking to me, but it

just electrifies me more. When the pulsing orgasm finally dies down, Michael takes his sticky fingers from my pussy and puts them to his lips.

He hasn't even taken his fingers back out when David leans forward and grabs my hips. He slides me forward just enough to bring his mouth to my pussy, and I sigh again into Michael's tight hand as David's tongue licks the cum off my lower lips.

He starts doing things with his tongue that I didn't know you could do down there. His tongue licks the honey from my lips and moves up to my clit, where it presses in and squirms around. It's torture--sweet, sweet torture that makes me start welling up with tension all over again.

Once I cum, it's so much easier for me to start cumming over and over again. I always thought it was something wrong with me, and I'm terrified of what they'll think when they find out.

His licking gets to a steady rhythm. He moves his tongue up my wet pussy until it finds my clit, and he moves it in a little circle there until I start squirming. I put my hands into his dark hair and hold on, and I start pushing my hips up into him, pleading with silent desperation while Michael torments my nipples.

My whole body is excited. I feel Michael's

flicking in my pussy while David licks, and I start squeezing my thighs together out of reflex.

But David's grip is strong, and he keeps my thighs apart while he works on me. My hip thrusts are grinding against Michael's cock, and I hear him start to groan while I David works me.

It doesn't take long at all for me to feel that familiar tension ready to snap, and in a few minutes, I bite my lip and let out another sharp sigh of relief as I cum on David's face, wave after wave of heat surging through my body sweetly.

"I think she's ready, Michael," David says.

"I've had a little too much fun here," Michael chuckles, pinching my ass. "Besides, you're ready. You first."

My eyes spring open. I'm about to just get passed around these guys like a toy.

Why do I feel so, so ready for this?

David reaches forward with unbelievable strength and lifts me up, and the look in his eyes is one of pure lust.

I lick my lips and try to channel Tiffany's confidence as much as I can. I drape my arms around his shoulders and lace my fingers behind his neck. Immediately, I feel his cock touch my lips, and a shiver runs up my back.

"Do you feel good about this, Amanda?" he asks, stroking my ass with his thumbs as he holds me up.

"Uh-huh," I say, nodding. I feel dumb, but I can barely form words, I feel so good. "Anything you want."

"Good girl," he growls, and he lowers me onto his cock.

I feel a sharp pinch that makes we yelp, but after that, I feel nothing but pure bliss. His crown is every bit as huge and fulfilling as it looked, and I sink all the way down to the hilt.

"Fuck," he groans, breathing onto my face. His breath smells like cinnamon, and his cologne is manly and strong like my dad's. "Not many girls can go all the way down, honey. You're good."

His approval makes me bolder, and I bite my lip. I start to move my hips up and down on his cock, and the look of pleasure on his face makes me feel so, so wet.

He puts a hand around the back of my head and brings me into a hot, fierce kiss as he starts bucking up into me.

In no time, we start working in tandem. His hips thrust up, and mine thrust down. David moves in a steady, unstoppable rhythm, and it's hard work keeping up. Now I know how it must feel to work for him.

But if this is how that feels, I want to get signed up immediately.

I feel my whole body start to get tense, but I want to hold it back. I screw up my face as we kiss, trying to hold back so much pleasure, but I want to get him off at the same time as me. I don't know how I'm able to think those things. It's so unlike me!

I was always a preppy girl. I never even thought that many dirty thoughts. But being on David's cock like this and realizing how much these huge, powerful men have wanted to claim me...it awakens something in me that's just as primal and base as what's in them.

"Just like that," David groans as he fucks me harder. I feel his thick cock touching every part of my inner depths. I feel him pulse and throb inside me, and the thought that he wants to release in me as bad as I want it is too much to bear.

"I'm gonna cum, David," I whimper, "I'm sorry, I wanted to make you cum with me!"

Something about my whimpering tone must have triggered something in David, because I feel his cock get stiffer and thicker than ever. He leans his head back and draws in a sharp breath as if he had just gotten burned, and then he brings his lips to mine in a hot, fierce kiss.

The next second, I feel his hot, thick cum shoot up into me, and it sends me spilling over the edge.

A full-body orgasm hits me, and I convulse and writhe on his cock. David shoots load after load of hot cum into my insides, plastering me with his pearly gold, and my squirming only gets more to come out.

I've never felt anything this thrilling. Getting more of that wonderful cum from his cock is better than anything I've ever tasted, and I want so much more.

David lets out a shuddering sigh when the last of his cum leaves him. My orgasm is still making me glow, and I open my eyes to give David a shy smile.

It's enough to earn me another spurt of his cum up inside me, and we both shudder before I melt onto his chest. He wraps his arms around me and strokes my hair gently, moaning softly.

I hear the sound of something moving behind me, and I turn my head to see that Michael has his cock out, working his shaft as he looks directly at me with a hungry gaze. It's like David isn't even there--all he sees is me, and I feel like a deer in the headlights.

"Hope you're not too tired, honey," David growls. "Because now, you're his."

I feel a rush of excitement run through me as David helps me off his cock, and his cum spills down his spear before Michael takes me from his hands. I'm getting passed around like a prize to be used, and that alone sends excitement through my body.

"I've got you," Michael coos as he takes my hips. I realize he's about to take me from behind, and I brace myself.

But nothing could have really prepared me for the feeling of his monstrously huge shaft filling me up in one swift, strong thrust.

I let out a shuddering cry of delight when he enters me. I don't know what Tiffany's time has been like, but she can't be having as much fun as I am.

Michael rips my remaining lingerie off and tosses it aside to make it easier for him to grope my breasts. He plays with them as if they were made just for him. He squeezes them one second and feels their weight the next, letting his thumbs explore the stiff nipples and toy with them idly.

He wastes no time in bucking up into me. While he does, David watches my bouncing breasts and starts touching himself, massaging his balls and shaft in the afterglow of his orgasm.

Michael reaches around to my front and starts fingering my clit while he bucks up into me. Each thrust touches a new, deeper part of my pussy at a whole new angle.

I never realized that a different position could feel different, but it's a whole new experience. Michael's swollen crown grinds against parts of my inner depths that David's cock couldn't get to from that angle, and I love every second of it.

I feel him pulsing and throbbing inside me, and I feel something wet deep inside that promises so much more. I'm slicker than I ever have been.

Although I'm ashamed to admit it, I've touched myself before, but nothing I've done on my own can compare to the kind of stimulation I'm getting from these men. I never knew that they always wanted to do this to me, but now, I couldn't be more happy that it's happening. I want to stay on Michael and David's cocks forever.

I know this is only for the job, but it feels so much better having known them before.

Michael touches my body lovingly, all over, and David is ravishing me with his eyes. Michael doesn't just touch my nipples and my clit, through one hand never leaves my clit, rubbing it in those same unstoppable circles. He touches my stomach, my shoulders, my thighs, anything he can reach.

His touch is so loving that I wonder just how much he's thought about this.

I start letting out little gasps with every thrust. His bucking is hard and strong, and every single one grinds up against a spot deep inside me that simply electrifies me. It's a stronger feeling than I've ever felt in my life.

I feel so bad for judging Tiffany for using sex toys now.

Nothing can hold back my moans as I feel another orgasm welling up in my body. Michael starts getting less regular, and he stops trying to maintain an even rhythm. He grabs my hips with both hands and holds on tight before he starts rutting into me like a wild beast.

I hear his rhythmic, gravelly grunting in my ear, paired with hot breaths each time he fucks up into me. It gets faster and faster, and I realize he's about to release himself inside me.

Just as he lets out a final groan and releases the first burst of cum inside me, I feel another orgasm hit me like a truck, shaking my thighs and spreading out to every finger and toe, bringing me close to passing out from the overwhelming feeling.

Michael empties himself into me, pouring out everything he has in thick, hot shots that just keep coming.

And when it's finally over, I'm a useless mess.

We sit there panting for longer than I can keep track of, and Michael never gets less stiff. His cock twitches inside me a few times before he finally pulls me out, and he lays me down on the couch between the two of them.

I can't even speak, I'm too worn out. My whole body shakes.

Michael takes my feet in his hands and massages them gently, while David does the same with my shoulders.

"You're a very talented young lady, Amanda," David says in a husky tone.

"Indeed," Michael says beaming down at me. I can barely keep my eyes open. "I think we might need to revisit what we said about tips."

"What do you mean?" I ask, a tiny twinge of fear hitting me. Was I not good enough?

"I mean," he says, leaning forward with a wolfish smile, "we should discuss keeping you around...permanently."

$\mathcal{F}$ive months later, life couldn't be better.

The only hard part was explaining to Dad why I was swelling up like a balloon with Michael and David's baby, but the feeling of that was so good that I didn't care.

The guys made good on their promise. I quit working at the club after one day, because I knew I didn't want any cocks filling me up by Michael and David's. They took me in and gave me anything I asked for.

And believe me, I tried to push the limits.

I never knew that one night getting pumped full of virile cum could be so life-changing, but it was the best choice I ever made.

The first thing I did was get Dad a promotion with a massive bonus, and on top of that, I got my parents a new house, car, and cleared all our family debts. After that, the men insisted that I get something for myself.

So, I took them up on their offer to get me a swanky apartment in downtown Boston. But they went a little further than that--they also got me one in Tokyo, one in Paris, and one in San Francisco, plus unlimited use of one of their private jets to go to any of them whenever I wanted.

There was only one condition: whenever either of them wanted me with them, I had to be there. And to me, that was just an added bonus.

The more pregnant I looked, the more they fawned over me, and after five months, they decided to take leave to see me through the rest of my pregnancy.

And that was when they proposed to me.

With two guys, two huge rings, and more money than I knew what to do with, I had everything a girl could possibly want or know what to do with.

Well, except one thing.

I still had to get Tiffany hooked up with the life of her dreams too, for being the one who started it all. That's going to be my birthday present to her next week.

And the look on her face is going to be priceless.

TEACHING HER

I can still see him so clearly in my mind's eye. Professor Jonathan Black, the sexy older man of my deepest, darkest fantasies. It hardly matters at all that I have known him since I was a little girl. In fact, that might even make him more attractive to me.

He is one of my father's closest friends and confidantes, and by all rights I should see him as more of an uncle, the kind of guy who is completely off-limits to me. But I can't help it: whenever I think about Professor Black, tall and broad-shouldered, wearing his usual gray tweed suit and tie, I can feel my body reacting in a very inappropriate way.

I can almost feel his big, strong hands sliding

down my body, cupping my breasts, slipping down between my legs. There I go again.

It hasn't always been like this, of course. In fact, even a year ago I might have been grossed out at the idea of fucking my dad's best friend. But something has changed inside of me in the past year. It's almost like the moment I turned eighteen, I suddenly learned what it feels like to desire someone… fiercely. To want him to touch me and kiss me and move me in ways nobody has moved me before.

And it just so happens that this is the worst possible time for me to develop such an irresistible crush, because this is my freshman year at Sunny Brook Women's College. I am a Sunny Brook girl through and through. All the women in my family have been alumni of this university for decades and decades. Hell, my father is even the head of the history department here. Growing up, I knew from day one that Sunny Brook was in my future. I have never wanted to go anywhere else. I was so excited to get my very first dorm room and move out of my parents' house across town. At first, they didn't want me to. I was nervous, too, but I'm eighteen now, and I need some freedom. Oh, and I definitely need more privacy.

Especially right now.

I am standing in the en suite shower I share with my roommate, trying to let the steamy water wash away the inappropriate thoughts and desires in my head. I need to focus. This year is so vital to my future: I have to make good grades. I have to make friends. I have to get accepted to the same sorority my mother, older sister, and aunts have been members of. This is crunch time, and I should not be wasting precious time and energy daydreaming about my hot professor. But my decision to take a shower has backfired, because I can't stop touching myself.

I close my eyes and let out a deep, slow sigh. I try to stop myself from thinking about Professor Black, but his image appears in my mind again and again. That steel-gray hair perfectly combed back. Those icy-blue eyes that seem to sear right through me to see my very soul underneath. Sometimes when I'm sitting in front of him in class, it is nearly impossible for me to even listen to a word he's saying. I try to take notes, but I just end up doodling and writing pure nonsense as I zone out, listening to his sexy growl. I know I can't be the only girl in class who fantasizes about him, but I am the only student of his whom he's known for over a decade. He has been to so many of our family dinner parties. Last summer, he came with us when my father took us out on his yacht. Yes. My daddy has a yacht. What can I say? I'm Connecticut royalty, a prep school princess with an old money pedigree. Which is why it's so messed up for me to be daydreaming about my professor. I'm supposed to be a good girl.

I cup my full breasts, sliding my fingers up over my slick, soapy nipples. A little gasp of pleasure escapes my lips. I've never touched myself like this before. I have never really felt the need to. A late bloomer, they call me. All throughout high school my classmates made dirty jokes and talked about hooking up, but I was only interested in playing soccer and going on hikes in the Connecticut forest. Sure, I had minor crushes here and there, but nothing like my overwhelming feelings for my teacher. I bite my lip, looking up at the detachable shower head as my heart pounds wildly. Do I dare? I've never tried it myself, but I've heard that it feels good.

The image of Professor Black looking right at me during a lecture comes to mind and I can feel my pussy getting wet between my legs, and not just from the stream of shower water. I take the detachable shower head and sit down on the smooth porcelain, holding my breath nervously as I position the spray between my legs. I close my eyes and start to relax a little, letting the steady stream of water massage my inner thighs before slowly, carefully moving the pulsing water to brush across my clit. I gasp and shudder with surprise at how intense the sensation is. It's almost too much to bear. I switch the setting to a softer pulse and shiver, getting goosebumps as the water dances over my virginal flower. I spread my thighs wider and begin to move the shower head in a tight, slow circle. I imagine Professor Black pushing me back onto his desk, lifting up my plaid skirt, and spreading my thighs. I can picture him licking and sucking at my clit, his tongue sliding up and down my slick little pussy while those icy blue eyes watch me closely. I moan and tremble, thinking of how he would hold me down, his hands gripping my waist while he devours my cunny, licking faster and harder until finally…

"Oh my gosh," I whimper, shuddering as a wave of powerful, indescribable pleasure shoots through my body. I lie there panting and heaving, totally overcome with awe at my first ever orgasm. I never knew it could feel that good. I know I should feel ashamed, but instead I just feel amazing. After I stop trembling, I stand back up and continue washing my hair and body, making a mental note to try that again soon. Now that I know how good it feels, I want to do it again and again. But I know I have to pace myself.

I get out of the shower and towel off, then check my cell phone which is sitting on the bathroom counter. To my surprise, I have a text message from one of the girls from Kappa Theta Nu! I hurriedly pick up my phone and read over the message.

Hey girl! Just so you know, there's going to be a lingerie slumber party tonight at the Kappa Theta Nu house. All our favorite pledges will be there, and you are one of the lucky chosen ones! Oh, and make sure you wear your sexiest panties, because we also invited some of the Sigma Pi guys. Party starts at seven! She included a winking emoji. I let out a squeal of excitement and check the time. It's nearly six o'clock already! I hastily blow-dry my hair, give myself a smokey eye and some red lipstick, and walk over to my dresser to take out the one and only set of lingerie I own. I bought it over the summer, thinking that since I was eighteen now, I needed to buy some grown-up stuff. I have never actually worn it before. I'm too shy. Besides, I don't have a boyfriend. Who would I wear it for?

Thankful that my roommate is out of town today, I slip on the lacy pink bra and matching thong panties, then pull on my thigh-high white stockings and a pair of cute pink kitten heels. I look at myself in the full-length mirror hanging on the back of the door and take a deep breath. I still feel kind of nervous wearing this. I mean, I'm a virgin. I don't know how to be sexy! But I must admit, looking at my reflection, I look pretty good. My long, dark-brown hair falls in soft waves down my back, my smokey eye makeup makes my cinnamon-colored eyes pop. Even though a year ago I had the body of a skinny teenage soccer player, over the summer my body has blossomed. I have full, soft breasts, a slender waist, and curvy hips with a tight little ass. I do a slow spin, blushing at the sight of myself in lingerie.

My phone chimes again and I see a text from another sorority girl named Trish I met at the meet and greet party they held a few weeks ago. *Hi Abby! Do you need a ride to the slumber party tonight? I can swing by and pick you up!*

"Oh, that's sweet," I murmur happily. I text her back, agreeing. I throw on a silky bathrobe and only twenty minutes later, Trish honks her car horn outside in the parking lot. Grinning from ear to ear, I rush outside and hop in her cute little Volkswagen bug. We chat about classes and sorority stuff on the ride there. Trish seems really nice, if maybe a little ditzy. When we get to the Kappa Theta Nu house, it's already getting dark outside. The sorority house is on campus, only about a hundred feet away from the history department building where my father's office is located. I try not to think about the fact that Professor Black's office is in there, too.

"Wait here, okay?" Trish says to me, her blonde ponytail bouncing as she turns back to smile at me. "I just need to check something. I'll come get you in a second."

"Oh. You want me to wait out there? In my... underwear?" I ask shyly.

"Yeah, silly! It'll just take a second. Don't worry," she says with a wink as she disappears into the sorority house. I wait outside, looking around the dark, quiet campus and hoping nobody sees me. I feel so exposed. So vulnerable. Several minutes pass, and I'm starting to get really nervous. I walk up to the front door and try to open it. The door is locked. I give it a few hard knocks. No answer. It's a little chilly out there, and I have goosebumps from waiting in the cold, barely dressed.

I send Trish a text, asking where she is, and her reply makes my heart sink.

Gotcha! Haha, welcome to day one of hazing. There is

no lingerie party, silly!

What am I supposed to do? I send back frantically.

Not my problem! Trish replies with a devil emoji.

"Oh my god. I cannot believe this is happening," I mutter. I glance over at the history building. If my dad looks out his office window, he'll see me here. If he catches his pure, innocent daughter standing outside in the cold in nothing but a lacy bra and panties, there will be hell to pay.

"I should've known this was too good to be true," I groan, wracking my brain for a way out of this awful situation. Just then, I see someone walking toward me out of the corner of my eye: a dark, tall figure coming from the direction of the history building.

"Oh no," I gasp, trying to duck behind a tree. What if it's my dad?

"Abby?" the male voice calls out. "Abby Collins?"

I recognize the voice instantly. But it's not my father's voice.

I peek around the tree, blushing. "Professor Black?" I whisper.

He comes strolling over with a concerned expression on his handsome face. My heart starts to race as he looks me up and down. He raises an eyebrow and I start to make excuses.

"I-I was tricked. They said there was a party tonight but they lied. They locked me out," I say hurriedly. "I didn't do this on purpose!"

"You know, if your father was to catch you out here, you'd be in big trouble," he says.

"I know, I know. But please don't tell him. He's so overprotective. He'd just make me move back home or something, and I'm eighteen! I need my freedom, you know?" I burst out, my lip trembling. "Please, please don't tell my dad. I-I'll do anything. I'll do extra credit or whatever else you want, I swear."

"Anything else?" Professor Black says coyly.

I nod vigorously, stepping closer to him. "Yes. Anything. Just don't tell my dad."

"Come with me," he commands in a low growl. He drapes his coat over my shivering body and leads me back toward the history building. My heart is pounding. Is he taking me to my father? I'm almost too afraid to ask. But he takes me to a back entrance, quietly guiding me into the elevator to the third floor. It's the same floor as my dad's office, but to my surprise, he doesn't take me to my dad. Professor Black leads me to a different room-- the Black Book Library. It's a room I have never been inside, a small library of Professor Black's rare and expensive book collection, which he donated to the school. It's a beautiful room with wood floors, a leather armchair, a gorgeous mahogany desk, and shelves upon shelves of books lining every wall.

"Wow," I murmur, looking around in awe. I turn to look back at my professor with confusion. "But why are we here?"

He walks up to me and takes my chin in his hand, peering into my face with those piercing blue eyes. I can hardly remember to breathe as he explains, "If you do as I say, I won't tell your father about what you were doing tonight. Abby, you aren't the same little girl you used to be. I would be a liar if I said I haven't noticed. You're turning into quite the beautiful young woman." He looks me up and down appreciatively. I feel a flicker of that same old desire.

"What are you saying?" I ask, eyes wide.

He gives me a sly smile. "I'm saying that tonight, you are going to help me act out a fantasy of mine." He walks over to the mahogany desk and opens a drawer, taking out a strip of black fabric. Professor Black comes back to me and ties the strip around my head, blindfolding me. I can hardly believe this is really happening.

"What are you going to do to me?" I whisper.

"My friend and I are going to fuck you. Right here in the library. With your father right down the hall. You will be quiet and do exactly as I tell you. Do you understand?" he says coolly.

I nod. "Yes, sir. I understand."

"Good girl," he replies. "Wait here."

I hear him walk away and open the door, his footsteps heading down the hallway as I stand blind-folded and overwhelmed. This has to be a dream, right?

A few moments later, the door creaks open and two sets of footsteps enter the room. I hold my breath, not knowing what to expect. The door closes and I hear someone lock it.

"Who's there?" I ask softly.

The next thing I know, there's a hand clapped over my mouth. A tall, powerful body slides up behind me, smelling of cologne and cognac. Professor Black. I can sense him, his hands roving down my body, groping and caressing my breasts. I tremble, unable to comprehend what's happening to me. A moment later, there's another man in front of me. He smells and feels different, yet familiar. I can't quite place it. I stand totally still while the second man leans in and presses his lips to mine. His hands cup my face as his tongue probes inside of my mouth. I've never been kissed before. The sensation of four hands touching me, the musky scent of two men pressing me between them, and the mystery man's lips against mine is enough to make me weak in the knees. I go almost totally limp, with my professor holding me up from behind. I can feel something long and hard pressing against my bare ass, and I realize with a jolt it's his cock.

Professor Black gropes my breasts through the thin lace of my bra, stroking my sensitive, perky nipples with his fingers. The mystery man in front of me has softer hands, moving slowly down my body, caressing my every curve. He slips a hand between my thighs, cupping my soft, aching mound in his palm. I feel a shiver of anticipation as he begins to gently stroke me through the lace of my panties, his fingers circling my clit while Professor Black squeezes my tits. I lean back against him and to my delight he begins kissing the ticklish, exposed flesh of my neck. I moan, starting to rock my body in tandem with the finger stroking my cunny.

Just when I think it can't get any better, he hooks his finger under the fabric of my panties and yanks them aside so he can gently slide a a digit inside of my pussy. I gasp, shocked at the sensation of his finger delving inside my tight hole, expertly stroking at a deliciously pleasurable spot deep within me. He moves faster and faster, fucking my pussy with first one finger, then two, then three. It almost hurts as he stretches my tight little hole, but it feels so fucking good.

Professor Black smacks my ass hard, making me cry out. Again, a hand comes up to cover my mouth. "Shhh," he growls in my ear. "Don't want your daddy to hear you."

The mystery guy kneels down in front of me and tugs down my panties. I let him take them off, wondering what will happen next. But nothing could have prepared me for the sensation of a warm, wet mouth licking and sucking at my clit. I whimper and shake as he lifts one of my legs up over his shoulder, diving in and devouring my pussy while Professor Black nips and sucks my neck, his hands still roughly groping my breasts. The mystery man slides his finger back inside me, fucking my tight cunny while he plays with my clit. It's not long before I'm coming, my whole body shuddering with the overwhelming pleasure.

"Good girl. Come all over his fingers," my professor hisses in my ear. "Such a good little slut. How long have you wanted a man's touch on your body? Tell me, Abby, have you touched yourself? Made yourself come?"

"Yes," I gasp. They never let up for even a second.

I hear my professor unzip his pants and then I feel his hard, massive cock pressing against my ass. I rut up against him, needing to feel him close to me.

He groans appreciatively and says, "Do you want this cock in your mouth, little girl?"

I nod. "Yes, sir. Please." Truthfully, I don't know what I'm doing, but I can't stop now.

The mystery man continues to fingerfuck my aching cunt, harder and faster while he sucks my clit, flicking his tongue over the sensitive little bud until I'm squirming.

"Come again for me," Professor Black snarls, his breath ticklish on my skin.

Like magic, my pussy gushes with sweet honey as I tremble and moan. The second man laps it up hungrily, lightly smacking my twitching cunt with his fingers. It hurts and feels incredible at the same time, and I have to bite my lip to keep from screaming.

"I've wanted this for so long," my professor growls, groping my ass and rubbing his cock against me. "I have been patiently waiting. Little Abby Collins. Always off-limits. But you're mine now. Get on your knees."

Both men let go of me and I kneel down, still blindfolded. I can feel my pussy dripping wet

CANDY QUINN

between my thighs as I wait for the next move. A pair of hands reach down and take off the blindfold. I blink slowly, letting my eyes adjust to the dim light of the lamp. In front of me stands Professor Black and a younger man with dark curly hair and gorgeous green eyes. He's tall and lanky, wearing a white t-shirt and jeans. Professor Harry Davis. He's the adjunct history professor all my classmates are in love with. He's only twenty-nine and boyishly good-looking. He's known as Professor Black's protege, and he's so cool he insists that his students call him Harry, instead of Professor Davis.

Both of them strip out of their clothes, and I gawk at their long, glorious cocks bare and impressive in front of me. Professor Black bends down and ties my hands behind my back, then stands up straight, looking down at me.

"Have you ever had a cock in your mouth, Abby?" he asks in a low, rough voice.

"No, sir."

"Do you *want* a cock in your mouth?"

I swallow hard, my mouth already salivating. "Yes, sir." I part my lips, looking up at them both expectantly. I'm a little scared, but I'm even more turned on. My professor gives Harry a subtle nod, and Harry takes a step closer, stroking his smooth, hard shaft.

"Come on," he says gently. I give the head of his cock a tentative lick, and the silver-haired professor cups the back of my head, pushing Harry's cock deeper into my mouth until I can feel the tip brushing against the back of my throat. I almost start coughing, but I get ahold of myself.

"Relax. It's okay," Harry assures me, stroking the hair back from my face. He gives me a soft smile and begins to slowly rock his hips, his cock sliding in and out of my mouth. As I get the hang of it, I begin to sukc harder, bobbing up and down on his cock and moaning at the sensation of my cheeks being stretched to accommodate his size. Harry groans, tilting his head back and closing his eyes while I suck his cock. All the while, Professor Black has a fistful of my hair, pushing me and controlling me so I can't push away. Not that I'd want to. I love the feeling of my mouth stuffed with cock, more than I ever expected I would. Professor Black is stroking his own shaft, watching me give his friend a blowjob. I can tell he's impatient for his turn.

Harry notices, as well, and withdraws. Professor Black steps up and shoves his massive cock into my mouth, pushing me down to the hilt until my eyes are watering. He groans and sighs as he holds my head, sliding in and out of my mouth faster and harder. He's a lot rougher than Harry, but I never want him to stop. I flick my tongue up and down the length of his shaft, whimpering with pleasure as he fucks my mouth.

"God, your mouth feel so good," he groans. He pushes back and Harry steps forward. I get the hint. I turn and suck Harry's cock for a few moments, then go back to my professor's, alternating between the two of them, sucking hungrily.

Just as I can feel them both getting closer and closer, their bodies tensing up, Professor Black steps away and snaps his fingers. "Stand up," he demands. I follow his command obediently, and he scoops me up in his arms, carrying me so easily I might as well have been made of feathers. He carries me over to the mahogany desk and sweeps all the papers and books onto the floor, cradling me back onto the desk He unties my wrists and scoots me back, then walks around to the other side. He tilts me back so that my head rests just on the edge of the desk, and then he shoves his cock down my throat as I lie here spread-eagled.

He fucks my throat hard and fast, his hands groping my breasts and tweaking my nipples, while

Harry walks over. He positions the head of his shaft at my slick, tight hole and begins to rub a slow, tantalizing circle, making me shiver. There's no time to ask questions. This is happening. In one swift, smooth movement, Harry slides his long, rock-hard shaft inside my aching cunny and I cry out. In response, Professor Black only fucks my mouth harder, keeping me quiet while Harry begins to pump in and out of my virgin pussy.

"Fuck, you're so tight," Harry hisses between gritted teeth.

"She's a virgin. Aren't you, Abby?" Professor Black says. I whimper with mingled pain and pleasure as the younger professor grabs hold of my hips, holding me in place while he rams his cock deep inside me, striking a deliciously blissful spot far within me, a place no one has ever touched. I'm rocked back and forth between them, the desk squeaking and scraping on the wood floors as the silver-haired professor fucks my throat and the curly-haired one thrusts inside my cunt. Harry reaches down to massage circles into my overly-sensitized clit while he pounds my pussy again and again, overwhelming me with waves of bliss. I moan and whimper, tears rolling down my cheeks as I come over and over again, gushing over Harry's cock while my cheeks ache from Professor Black's shaft down my throat.

"Yes, yes," growls Professor Black. "Come for teacher, sweet little Abby."

I'm exhausted, my body trembling and over-whelmed. Finally, they both back off, but only for a second. Professor Black picks me up again and carries me over to the armchair, where he sits down and lowers me onto his lap, straddling him.

"Harry's going to put his cock in your tight little virgin ass," Professor Black snarls, rutting against me with animalistic need. "While I fuck that beautiful pink cunt."

I hold my breath with fear. I have heard from other girls that anal is painful. Unbearable. But Harry reaches into a desk drawer and pulls out a tiny bottle of lube. He squirts it into his hand and rubs it in tight little circles around my asshole, care-fully and slowly sliding the tip of his finger inside while Professor Black lowers me down onto his cock, spearing me from below. I tremble and whim-per, rolling my hips and riding him as Harry cautiously presses the head of his cock against my ass. He spends a good few minutes working me up to it, and I find myself a little impatient toward the end, wishing he would just fuck me. I can't believe how quickly I've transformed from a shy little virgin to a cock-hungry slut.

Finally, Harry eases the head of his cock into my ass, making me whine and moan as Professor Black fucks my pussy harder and faster. He slams up into me, leaning forward to suck and nip at my breasts while he pounds my cunt. Behind me, Harry is slowly gaining momentum, filling my tight little ass with his massive shaft. Before long, both men are fucking me hard, ramming into both of my holes so quickly and roughly all I can do is wrap my arms around the older professor and hold on for dear life. It's an overwhelming sensation. Harry's cock in my ass hurts so good, adding a level of pleasure and pain that makes me lose control, while Professor Black slams into my g-spot again and again, both of them moving in tandem to bring me closer to the brink. I shudder through another orgasm, this time so overcome with pleasure that I let out a scream. Professor Black dives forward and kisses me hard, swallowing my scream and silencing me as my pussy explodes, slicking down his cock and dripping all over the leather upholstery. The two men don't give me even an inch of mercy, thrusting into my tight little holes so hard I'm seeing stars. I remember that my stern, overprotective father is in his office just down the hall. The door is locked, but there is a small glass window in the door. If he was to walk by and look inside, he would see his precious, innocent little girl getting fucked in her ass and pussy by two of his most esteemed colleagues.

But that realization only turns me on even more. The danger, the knowledge that we could get caught at any second only adds fuel to the fire. I roll my hips, clenching my pussy and moaning. I want both men to come inside me. I want to milk every last drop of their seed. I don't even care that I'm not on birth control yet. All I want is to make these two sexy, strong, powerful men shoot their honey inside my holes. It's like the older professor can read my mind.

"I'm going to fill your little cunny with my come, Abby. Do you like that? Do you like the thought of my seed leaking out of your pussy? I bet it turns you on, doesn't it?" he snarls.

"Yes, yes, yes!" I gasp, riding him harder while Harry slams into my ass.

"What would your daddy think of his little girl right now? A cock in her ass and her cunt. What a dirty little slut you are," he hisses, holding me in place while he thrusts up into me. I can feel Harry starting to lose control behind me, moaning and rutting into me erratically.

"Please, come inside me. I want it. I need it," I whimper.

Harry's the first to explode, gripping my hips so tightly it stings while he pumps my ass full of hot, sticky come. A moment later, Professor Black lets out a loud, shuddering groan, shooting his load deep inside my convulsing pussy. Both men caress and kiss me all over as I collapse forward onto the older professor's chest, heaving and sighing. In the after-glow, they both help me get dressed, kissing and holding me with genuine affection throughout the process. Harry gives me his white t-shirt, which hangs on me almost like a short dress. The silver-haired professor drapes his coat back around me, and the two of them quietly sneak me back out of the building, undetected by my father.

~

Six months later, it's safe to say that I couldn't possibly care less about the sorority I tried to join. After that first night of hazing, I decided the sorority life was just too imma-ture for me. Besides, why in the world would I want to live with a bunch of silly girls when I can live with two sexy, distinguished professors instead?

That's right. For the past six months, I have been meeting up with Professor Davis and Professor Black in secret. We have fucked each other in the car, in their respective offices, even finding quiet places around campus, right in plain sight. I guess you could say we kind of get off on the sneaking around. For a while, that was enough. Just seeing each other under the cover of night, under the pretense of some lie. Sitting in class, listening to Professor Black talk about Western Civ, giving me that icy blue stare... it was hard to keep pretending we had a normal teacher-student relationship. Harry and I would meet up, too. In coffee shops. In the park. At his house. As soon as the semester ended and I was no longer a student of Professor Black's, we made it official: all three of us. We began going on real dates, in public places. In the daylight. At first, we still hid it from my parents. After all, my dad would be so betrayed.

Or so we thought. But just a few weeks ago, he retired from his position as head of the history department, and Professor Black took the job. Harry has been hired on as a full-time professor now, and I have decided to study biology.

Which means I am no longer a student of either professor. So finally, just last night, we broke the news to my parents that all three of us are moving in together. Professor Black recently bought a big, three-story Victorian house on the edge of the forest, close to all my favorite hiking trails. It's a fixer-upper, but the three of us are up to the job. And my parents aren't even angry! In fact, Daddy is kind of relieved to see that I'm dating two distinguished, brilliant, respectable guys. Sure, it might be a little awkward to see his best friend dating his daughter, but in the end, it's my decision. I'm old enough and smart enough to know what I want-- and there's no time to waste, because I'm pregnant! I'm going to have a son, and he will be the luckiest boy in the world, having two amazing fathers to help raise him. It will be a lot of work, being a full-time student and a young mom, but I can't imagine doing this with anyone else. My two sexy older men are going to take care of me. They love me passionately, and I love them. I wouldn't have it any other way.

ROCKING HER

I can't believe this is really happening!

My heart races as the bouncer leads me backstage. My ears are still ringing from the blaring music that everyone at the venue was jamming to just a few minutes ago. This band has been changing my life since I turned 18, and now, I'm actually going to meet them in person.

I'm wearing nothing but sandals, short shorts, and a thin white t-shirt that you can see my nipples through. My curly blonde hair is a mess thanks to how much hype the band whipped up on stage, but my pink lipstick is still glossy and perfect. My shining blue eyes are full of excitement, and I just *know* my cheeks are an even darker pink than my lips.

The sway of my shirt makes my nipples feel excited and stiff--my bra was long gone. I launched it on stage strapped to a tennis ball. I still can't believe nobody noticed it was me who threw it.

Everything else about tonight has been a disaster. Before the show, I thought my boyfriend was going to pop my cherry in his car to one of their songs, but instead, he dumped me for a job offer in another city. I wanted to cry my eyes out to my friends, but they got distracted by their own guys and left me all alone.

So I said fuck it.

I danced and went crazy in the crowd all on my own, and I had a great time.

I didn't realize my ticket had a raffle number on it, and I never for a second thought they'd call the number after the show and ask me to come backstage and meet the band.

But when the bouncer pushes the door open and leads be backstage proper, I know this is all real, not some wild dream.

My eyes go wide when I see the four of them standing there, larger than life. Grant McAllister, the vocalist, is standing there with his shock of gorgeous blonde hair and scruffy beard, his signature tattoos crawling up his thick arms from his wrists to his exposed biceps that look even bigger and more defined up close. Next to him is Lee Chambers, the drummer whose forearms look so strong he could pick me up with one hand. He's as gruff as Grant, with rich, thick, curly brown hair that melds with his beard, and better yet, he's already shirtless, showing off the elaborate ink that runs from his neck and all down his torso.

Jenna and Tyler Farley are there too, the lead guitarist and bassist respectively--the brunette and redhead have been married for years. They're great, but Grant and Lee have been on posters on my walls since I first heard the band perform.

And as the bouncer nods to me, I hurry forward, my stomach full of butterflies. What do I even say?! How am I supposed to act? A hundred thoughts race through my head as I nervously present myself before the four...

...and when they all turn to look at me, their reaction couldn't be more unexpected.

Grant and Lee's eyes go wide. Grant looks me up and down with ravenous eyes, and my face goes red as a cherry when I see Lee's face split into a wolfish grin.

"Um...hi!" I say. I can't think of a single other thing to say.

"Hey," Grant says in a voice as smooth as silk and thick as smoke. "If you're lost, don't worry, you're in the right place now."

My stomach does a somersault, and I bite my lip.

Jenna rolls her eyes. "She won the raffle, dickhead, she's here to meet us."

"Oh!" Grant says, chuckling. It's kind of a relief to see him taken off-guard, but he and Lee are so tall that they still seem to dominate the room, no matter what. Grant steps forward and sticks out a hand.

"Well then, congrats. I'm Grant, this is Lee, Jenna, and Tyler. Been a fan long?"

"Oh my god," I say, hardly able to contain my excitement as I feel Grant's massive hand cover mine and shake it before I shake everyone else's. "I-I-I...yeah! I'm Stacy. I've been a fan since high school!"

"She sounds almost as starstruck as you two," Tyler says, chuckling. He puts his arm around Jenna, and the two give each other a knowing look. "Hey, Stacy, me and Jenna are going to hit the bar, think you'll be okay getting to know Grant and Lee a little better?"

I don't know if my face can get any redder.

"Y-yeah, that sounds good," I say, and Grant and Lee can't keep the grins off their faces as they look me up and down.

I can't believe this. I've heard about how bands like to get a little friendly with fans after the shows like this, but I always thought it was kind of an exaggeration.

"Those two will be a while," Lee says as Tyler and Jenna walk off, arm in arm.

"Enjoy the show?" Grant asks.

"Oh my god, are you kidding?" I gush. I'm unable to hold anything back. My head is still spinning, partly just because this is *them*, and partly because of how they're looking at me. I notice Lee's brow furrow, and he crosses his arms. I suddenly realize he's staring at my chest.

"Hey, I got a question," he says, and he reaches into his back pocket.

To my horror, he pulls out my bra, still bearing the tape I used to attach it to a tennis ball. My eyes go so wide I'm worried they'll fall out of my head.

"This yours, or do you just like going braless?" he asks, and Grant's face lights up too.

"I...um...oh gosh," I murmur, and I start twirling a lock of my hair around my finger. "Well I didn't realize I'd be meeting you, and-"

"I think she's a real fan, Grant," Lee says.

"I think so too," he agrees before looking back down at me. "Gotta say, we've had a lot of shit thrown up on stage, but that was creative. How about a tour of the trailer? We've got some better beer in there."

I hardly have time to stammer a response before Lee scoops me up in his arms. I squeal a giggle as he hoists me up onto his shoulders, my legs around his neck, and I hold onto his hair and press my hips into the back of his head.

"Night's young," Grant chuckles. "Let's get out of here."

~

I squeal in delight as Lee tosses me onto the bed in the trailer, and my tiny frame bounces under the dim lights overhead.

The trailer is huge. I've never been inside one of these things before, much less known what they look like on the inside. It's like a luxury camper, full of band merchandise, liquor, and equipment strewn all over the place. It feels like one big messy bedroom, and I love it.

Not as much as I love what's happening with the guys who just carried me inside.

"So they just ditched you?" Grant asks, talking about my friends. We made a little chit-chat on the walk to the trailer, and I'm surprised to find out they're pretty down to earth people. "Jesus, they sound like dicks."

"I mean, I guess they're entitled to having fun," I say modestly.

"Still," Lee says, "leaving a cute little thing like you all on your own? That's criminal."

I giggle and curl up on the bed, batting my lashes at the two of them. They're stalking toward me with a hungry and playful look in their eyes, and it's making me more excited by the second.

"Yeah," Grant says, putting a knee on the bed and looming over me. "There are shady guys around here. Never know what could happen."

I'm starting to second-guess myself about dreaming.

At only 5' tall, I'm hard to spot in a crowd, much less notice. But these guys have been ravishing me with their eyes every second. Riding on Lee's shoulders on the way over here, Grant kept gazing at my legs--gazing, not glancing.

These men know what they like, and it turns out, I'm it.

I'm like prey for them, and *oh my god*, I never thought I'd enjoy it this much.

And that makes me a little bolder than I usually would be.

My big blue eyes move from one to the other. The trailer smells like beer and old clothes, but in a comforting way, and my sweet-smelling perfume that left glitter on my neck and arms stands out in sharp contrast.

"And just what might happen to a girl like me?" I ask, my voice full of anticipation.

To my surprise, Grant slips his hand around the back of my head, lacing his fingers through my curly locks and turning my head up to look at him. His eyes are full of simple, lustful desire.

"You might run into guys like us."

"Guys?" I ask, a smile curling my lips. I put emphasis on the plural. *Which one of them is going to want to have some fun with me?*

"Guys," Lee agrees, and he joins us on the bed, both of the huge men looming over me now. "We're a band, after all. We work best together. Are you that kind of fan?"

"Am I...?" I breathe, nearly laughing. My heart is fluttering in my throat, and I can barely breathe. "I...might have given it a thought or two."

"A thought, huh?" Grant asks, sitting down on the

bed next to me. "Don't tell me you still have your top on when you get these thoughts, do you?"

He reaches behind me and takes hold of my shirt, and before I can stop him, he lifts it up over my head, leaving me completely topless. I giggle and cover my chest, but I'm grinning at them like a schoolgirl.

"Or pants," Lee says, and he grabs my tight shorts and unbuttons the top. Next thing I know, Grant swings his leg over me and pushes me down on the bed, and he takes my arms and pries them off my chest to pin them down on the mattress.

I squeal, but I can't stop laughing.

I'm a nervous laugher.

After I'm pinned under grant, I feel my shorts leaving me as Lee pulls them down past my knees and off my feet. He takes my sandals next, leaving me totally naked.

"Sounds like you *are* that kind of fan," Grant growls as his big, rough hands start undoing his belt. He pulls the leather off and tosses it aside, and I realize there's a colossal bulge under his pants, so tight that it's threatening to burst out.

"Only in my dreams," I confess, biting my lip and squirming.

I feel Lee on my legs, his huge hands running up

and down the soft skin and squeezing it. "Let's make a dream come true, Grant," Lee's deep voice rumbles. Grant pulls a hair tie out of his pocket and ties his shaggy locks back, and he rips his shirt off, revealing a rippling, muscular body underneath the tank top.

I suck in a breath. I've touched myself plenty of times thinking about Grant's rock-hard body, but I never knew it was *this* ripped.

"How does that sound to you?" Grant asks.

The question isn't even out of his lips all the way before I start bobbing my head, making Grant chuckle.

"Do you do this...a lot?" I ask, almost afraid to.

Grant puts a hand to my face and runs his thumb over my lip. "Stacy," he says, and I'm amazed he remembers my name after hearing it just once. "I've never met a fan who's as down to share as we are, I can tell you that."

"Seriously?" I half-laugh. "How is that not, like, everyone's dream?"

Both the guys let out a hearty laugh, and Grant puts both hands around my face, bending way down to kiss me.

My heart pounds in my chest as he does. His beard tickles my face and neck, and I push my hips up in desire. When he finally breaks the short kiss, he whispers, "I think we're going to like you, Stacy."

I open my mouth to answer, but only a gasp comes out, because I feel fire between my legs.

Lee has gripped my thighs and put his face between my legs, and his long, hot tongue runs up my slit. It goes all the way to my clit, and it teases at the hooded nub. Somehow, the way he moves his tongue is just like the way I move my fingers over my clit when I have time to play with myself, but it's so much better.

The fire between my legs gets hotter with each time that he lets his tongue out to play with my clit. He starts off in a little circle, then brings his tongue down to the rest of my pussy to run it up the whole length of it. Each time he does, he spends a little time at my clit, back and forth.

Soon, he gets greedier, and the thick tongue dives further into my pussy. He tastes my honey for the first time, and he lets out a groan of delight.

"I like her a *lot*," he pauses to growl, and I feel a shiver run up my whole body.

Grant smiles down at me. "Lee's picky. You're a special girl, aren't you, Stacy?"

"I'll be whatever you want me to be," I gush, and Grant bends down to put his lips to me again.

"You just be you," he tells me, and he invades my mouth again.

While Lee lavishes my pussy with attention, Grant's tongue delves into my mouth. My tongue welcomes him in, dancing with him just past my teeth and feeling his warmth all around me. Everything about him gets me hot, from the breath washing over my face to the way he tastes like whiskey and smells like *man*.

While we kiss, his hands rub my arms up and down, warming my whole body and making me feel loved.

My ex-boyfriend never touched me like this. He was too much of a wuss.

Grant is so tall that he has to push himself back up when he moves his hands closer down. My mouth hangs open for a second after his lips leave me. I almost feel disappointed, but when I open my shining eyes and get to see him looming over me just as Lee touches my clit with a firm, strong touch, I feel warm all over.

Grant winks down at me, and before I can say anything, he puts his hands on my breasts.

I lean my head back and groan as I feel so many hands on me at once, all working to make my body feel so fucking good.

Grant's palms feel me up, squeezing my breasts and testing them, and he lets out a soft, rumbling groan as he savors the feeling. I push my chest up to give him more, letting him explore every part of me he wants.

I've always been kind of a party girl, but I've never done anything like this.

While Grant roams over my breasts, getting my nipples so stiff that it almost hurts, Lee is being merciless with my pussy.

His tongue delves deep into it, then comes up to torture my clit like a surge of electricity. He groans into it, licking faster and faster until it feels tense down there. My head is swimming, and their music is swirling through my mind the whole time.

"Fuck," I groan, grasping the sheets under me while the guys have their way with me slow and steady. "Is this really happening?"

"You tell me," Grant chuckles, and he takes his hands off my breasts to unbutton his pants and open them.

His cock springs free, and the sight of it makes me so hot that I feel my whole body come to attention.

Grant's shaft is a long, thick pillar that sticks straight out, ribbed with veins. His crown is dark red, and it's bulging so much that it must be uncomfortable for him. His heavy balls come out of his pants next, and they're so huge that just the thought of the thick, potent cum in them gets me wetter for Lee.

I hear Lee groan down between my legs--he hasn't stopped this entire time. He must be starving for pussy. That, or mine is just irresistible.

"I think she likes what she sees, Grant," he pauses to say, and he rewards me with a long, delicious stroke of my pussy that brings me so close to the brink that I could swear I'm about to cum.

"I- ah! I've never seen one before," I confess in a whimpering tone. "Not in person, at least."

"Really now?" Grant says, and he strokes his shaft with his huge hand while massaging one of my breasts with the other. He then starts to lower his cock to my mouth, and my eyes go wide. "Then tell me what you think."

He comes down so fast that I just let my mouth fall open in surprise, but the next second, my lips are full of my idol's cock.

The second my tongue touchest the bulging crown, I spill over the edge, and I let out a high-pitched whimper and clench my thighs around Lee's head.

Honey floods Lee's face as warmth radiates out from my clit and lower abdomen to the rest of my body, rolling out like little spirals that heat up every limb. I tense up and relax, throbs of beautiful, exciting heat consuming my body.

My soft sighs are like music as I start licking Grant's cock like a lollipop, lavishing it with as much attention as Lee has been giving my pussy.

The first orgasm a man ever gave me...and it's from none other than the drummer whose songs have been in my head for years. I'm in heaven.

"Woah," Grant chuckles between groans as I start taking more and more of his cock into my mouth. "I know that sound. And I know a virgin when I feel one."

My eyes spring open, and I take his cock out of my mouth to give him a worried look, batting my eyelashes at him. "Is that not okay?"

Grant laughs, brushing a lock of hair out of my face. "Oh honey, it's great, don't you worry."

I smile and take his cock back into my mouth, and this time, I get bolder. I take half of his cock in, using my tongue to press it against the roof of my mouth while I feel the soft underside of his cock. But I don't stop there. I reach up the sides of his shaft with my cock and keep taking more and more of him into me, and all the while, Lee keeps massaging my clit with his tongue, guiding me through the orgasm.

Grant lets his head fall back, groaning while I play with his cock. Now that I've got one in my mouth, I understand all the craze about it.

I don't just like cock. I love it, and I never want to go without one close by.

I feel a drop of precum in my mouth, just like all the dirty books I read talk about. That encourages me, and I start getting bolder with my attention. Every now and then, I bring my tongue up to the very tip of his cock and tease the slit with it, coaxing out a little more precum each time. Grant takes a fistful of my hair and squeezes it gently, just to show that he still has control over me, but I'm excited now.

Just when I start to feel Grant's cock pulsing in my mouth, and idea comes into my head, and I slowly, reluctantly take it out of my mouth, making sure to run my tongue long and hard along his shaft.

When the tip of his cock leaves my mouth, Grant looks down at me in confusion. "Something wrong?"

"Fuck, no," I breathe. "I just want a little more. Can I?"

It takes Grant a second to realize what I mean

but then, his face splits into a grin. "Someone likes cock, huh? Lee, I think she wants to thank you for all your hard work."

"Mhmm," I whimper, nodding my head.

Grant swings his leg over me and stands up while Lee does the same. The two men start undressing in front of me, kicking their shoes off and pulling their pants down.

Lee is even more tattooed than Grant, and his ink is like art on a canvas of his body, even on his thighs. His cock is circumcised, and it looks just as delicious as Grant's. I put my fingers to my clit and start massaging myself with one hand while touching my breast with the other while I watch them.

"Alright, fangirl," Lee chuckles, watching the show and massaging his cock. "Show me how you wanna thank me."

I bite my lip, mind racing. I haven't thought this through, so I just act on pure instinct. I get on my knees and turn around, pushing my ass up toward him and looking over my shoulder at him with wide eyes, offering him my ass and the glistening-wet pussy under it.

"H-how's this?" I say nervously, genuinely unsure.

Lee's cock is stiffer than it was a few seconds ago, and his eyes are hazy with desire.

"Yeah, I think that'll do," he says in a husky tone, and he steps forward to grab my hips and put the tip of his cock against my wet lips. "Want me to go easy, baby?"

"I want you to give it everything you've got," I say, and I can barely believe my words.

"She's brave," Grant muses, and when I feel Lee's strong grip around my hips, I know he's right. Lee feels up my ass likes he owns it, massaging the soft flesh and reaching around to finger my clit a little while he gets comfortable on the bed. My blue eyes flit to Grant's cock, and I lick my lips hungrily.

"I want that, too," I plead, nodding to his cock.

"Damn, girl," Grant says, moving around to the other side of the bed and climbing up onto it. "Braver than I thought."

"She put some real thought into getting that bra on the stage," Lee growls. "What else did you expect?"

Grant gets his cock into position in front of my lips while Lee's is perched on top of my pussy. The wait is killing me--both of them are just a hair's breadth away from penetrating me from both sides, and my whole body is quivering in excitement.

Grant looks down at me and pets my head lovingly, letting out a low, long groan at the sight of me. "I think we might just have to keep you around," he says.

"Don't tease me," I whisper into his cock.

"I don't tease unless I mean it," he growls, and he brings his hand down to my jaw and squeezes it open gently.

The second his crown touches my tongue, Lee penetrates me.

Grant's cock in my mouth muffles my sharp cry of pain, but after that first pinch, I feel pure bliss. Lee's cock feels so different from Grant's, but it's incredible in all the right ways. I feel his bulging crown push its way through my virgin pussy that's been untouched by anything else that deep.

I was always too shy to get sex toys. Now, I realize what I've been missing out on this whole time.

He touches parts of me I've only dreamed of touching. His cock roves deep into me, and the way my hips are twisted to let him in, he grinds against a spot deep inside me that makes my whole body come alive with energy.

Somehow, instinctively, I know that's my g-spot,

and my eyes roll up into my head as I start tonguing Grant's cock.

As my tongue feels up every inch of Grant's massive shaft, I picture Lee's going deeper and deeper into my pussy. Just as Grant pulls his back, so does Lee, and both the men start pumping into me in a slow, steady rhythm. I don't know how my mouth compares to my pussy, so I start giving Grant as much work as I possibly can.

My tongue starts at the slit of his cock, then goes to the rim of his crown and down the soft underside of his cock. I feel that part of him pulsing more sensitively than the rest of him, and I push the tip of my tongue against it lovingly.

I could spend all day on his cock.

It goes all the way back to my throat, and when it hits the back, I hold back my gag reflex to give him the best experience possible. At the same time, I feel Lee's cock so far into me that I didn't even know it *could* go that far.

Lee's thrusting gets faster, and he starts getting rougher with me, both pulling my hips back into him while bucking up into me. Each time, he runs across my g-spot, and each time he does, I let him know by groaning into Grant's cock. I reach up and take Grant's balls in my hand to start massaging them gently, and the thought of him emptying those heavy, sore balls into my mouth makes me so wet that Lee's bucking gets faster.

"Just like that," Grant groans in a throaty husk. "Don't stop, Stacy!"

The encouragement is like sugar on my tongue, and I obey. In fact, I go an extra step and start clenching my pussy around Lee's cock as I get thrust back and forth between the guys, getting faster and faster.

Lee starts grunting with each thrust, and it doesn't feel like fucking anymore--it feels like rutting, nothing but savage *use* of my body, and it presses all the right buttons for me in ways I can barely describe.

There's something primal about it, and I realize something terrifying and exciting all at once: neither guy is wearing a condom, and I'm not on the pill.

And weirdly enough, I love that.

I want both these guys to fill me up, and I want it badly. I want that virile, heavy seed to plaster my insides, and I want even more than that.

I want them to knock me up.

That thought alone triggers something inside me, and I grip the sheets with my fists as my whole body starts to quiver.

I cum, hard. Heat shoots up my body, from my pussy to my chest, and I let out a long, delighted moan into Grant's cock as I lose all restraint, lavishing his cock with my tongue, desperate for its payload. The orgasm shakes my whole body, and I feel warm all over. If two cocks weren't holding my tiny body up, I'd be collapsing on the bed in a quivering mess.

Grant grabs my hair, harder this time, and I feel his cock pulsing and throbbing in a new way. His balls start to tighten in my hand, and I realize that I'm about to get my wish.

At the same time, I feel Lee in my pussy doing the same, and my body readies itself for what's about to come.

Grant pulls his cock out of my mouth with a wet pop, and I open my eyes just in time to watch his slit release a thick, hot shot of cum onto my face. It hits my cheek, and a second hits my lips, and after that, I lose track of where the shots start to hit me. My mouth can't stop smiling as Grant unloads his burden on me, load after load of cum dousing my face and running down in sweet, sticky drops.

I'm so lost in the sensation that Lee's first shot takes me by surprise. It coats my pussy in the first shot, and by the third, I lose track of how many he releases into me. I'm heavy with his cum, from the deepest depths to the very edge of my pussy. I feel some of the hot white fluid spill out and run over my clit, and I shudder with another little orgasm that ripples through my body.

Finally, the two guys pull out of me, and I collapse on the bed, panting and desperate as cum runs off me at both ends. Through thick, husky groans, they massage their cocks and let out a little more on each side of me before they're totally spent.

It's so strange and sweet, hearing those voices I've listened to so much through speakers now huffing and panting over me, satisfied.

And I'm the one who satisfied them. I can't keep the smile off my face.

"Fuck," Grant moans. "That was...Jesus, that was incredible."

"Yeah," Lee says between breaths. He reaches out and rolls me over, making my cum-drenched form look up at both of them lovingly. "I think that means we want to keep you around, babe. What do you say?" He flashes a grin at me. "Want to go on tour?"

*E*ight months ago, if you'd told me I'd be spending Christmas backstage at a stadium in Paris watching my two lovers perform before a crowd of hundreds of thousands, I'd have told you you were insane.

And if you'd have told me I'd be so pregnant that I looked ready to pop at any second, I'd have slapped you across the face.

But as I listen to the heavy drum beat and the sweetest voice in the world out there rocking the stage, I can't help but feel like this has still been all one big dream.

Grant and Lee kept me to themselves, just like they promised. We got to talking after our first night together, and it turns out that all three of us have had this thing for menages that we've never gotten a chance to explore. After breaking that ice, it was like we'd all known each other for years.

The two guys treat me like a queen. I've had nothing but the best food, clothes, and cars ever since we got together. And every night, I get the best thing out of all of it--the two of them, feeling me up and touching every part of my body together.

Every inch of my body has had their lips on it at one point, and I've been drenched in their cum more times than I can count. Sometimes we just go for as many times as we can in a single day, but each time, we lose track of it before we can figure out whether we set a record.

The guys were popular when we got together, but now, they're world class. There's a new spring in their step and new energy to their minds. Grant and Lee always say it's because I'm in their lives now.

I don't want to flatter myself by saying that's true, but regardless, I feel pride swell up in my chest every time I look at the charts and see their band rocking the top 10.

Life is good.

And it's only going to get better from here.

TRADING FOR HER

I can feel the burn of ropes around my wrists, burning into my soft skin, scraping like claws when I make even the slightest attempt to move my arms. It aches all the way down from my wrists to my shoulders, and I can feel my body starting to cramp up from sitting in this tense position for so long.

My legs are shoved widely apart, my pussy wet and glistening with need. My wrists are bound with cords to the bed posts, keeping me wide open and vulnerable, just a delicate prey for the predators stalking on either side of the bed.

Two men, tall and strong, with bulging muscles and hard, long cocks like spears stand over me, looking down at me as though they could dive in and devour every inch of my exposed flesh at any moment. I feel just the slightest shiver of fear, but the fear only adds to the anticipation, the desperation swelling up inside of me.

I need them to touch me. I need them to lay their huge, rough hands on my skin and move and bend me as they please. I want them to mark me up, use me, treat me however they want to, fill me up with their fingers, their cocks, their cum. I want to be stuffed full, I want to be fucked until I can't breathe or think straight.

I only wish I could see their faces.

But they move about in swaths of shadow, the darkness falling over their faces whenever I try to strain my eyes to get a better look. Faceless and powerful, they are almost more like beasts than men. Wild animals poised to rip me to shreds, tear me apart and feast on me like the tempting morsel I am.

I can hear my own heart beating loudly in my ears, the blood rush in my veins that I know they can hear, they can smell. I wonder if my fear exhilarates them, turns them on like it turns me on. I have never wanted anything so badly as I want these two faceless men. It's a need that burns and rages within me. I can't ignore it. I can't push it back down. I need them to fuck me. Now.

I open my mouth to whimper, to beg them.

"Please," I manage to choke out, but it's softer than a whisper, like all the air has been sucked out of my lungs. Still, my two suitors understand me perfectly, and they descend on me like animals.

Four hands, rough and calloused, roving up and down my soft, shivering body. I moan as two hands close over my full, perky breasts, sliding his thumbs up and over my nipples until they stand erect and sensitive to his every touch. He's groping me, caressing me, seizing my breasts like they belong to him. Like every part of me belongs to them. He leans down to pull my nipple into his mouth, flicking his tongue over it so that I'm gasping and moaning.

The other man is caressing my taut stomach, manhandling my hips, squeezing and tracing his fingers along my trembling thighs. He's teasing me. Playing with me as though I'm a toy. He knows how badly I need him without even asking.

Both of them can see right through me. I feel like they can read my minds, pushing into even the darkest, most cobwebby corners of my mind to seek out my deepest, most hidden fantasies.

They can tell what I want before I even know it fully myself, anticipating my every sigh and whimper. The second man pushes my thighs even further apart, climbing onto the bed to lower himself down and breathe in my special womanly scent, which sets me apart.

I bite my lip, looking down at him with my breath caught and held in my throat. I'm afraid to move, for fear that either one of them will stop touching me. I need them to keep touching me. I feel like I will fall apart the second they let go of me.

The first man bends down to kiss me, even though I still cannot see his face. But he finds my lips easily, and I sigh into his soft, warm mouth. He kisses me gently at first, more placating and calming than pushing.

But then he probes his tongue into my mouth and I allow him gladly, straining up to meet him, hoping he won't pull away. He gently bites my lower lip, making me shiver appreciatively. The second man is kneeling down on the bed, his face nestled between my legs. I feel his tongue lightly slide up and down my slick folds.

"Mmm," he growls, nuzzling into my cunt. It sends a vibration up through my body and I feel the pleasure begin to mount higher and higher.

They begin to speak to me in low, raspy voices. Guttural hums and growls that sound like speech but I can't quite decipher it, as hard as I try. And really, it doesn't matter. The words don't have to make sense to me to know what they're talking about: me. My body. How much they enjoy touching me and bringing me closer and closer to the edge…

Until I wake up with a start, my eyes opening wide to the blazing pillar of dawn's light streaming in through the window. I roll over in bed, slowly waking up out of my unfinished dream. I wonder what woke me up. I was so close to a release. I can't help but feel cheated out of something. Then a little bird on the tree branch outside my window starts his cheerful little song and I realize *that* is what woke me up.

"Ugh, you little bastard," I groan. "I needed that dream."

I close my eyes tightly again and try to will myself back to sleep, hoping I can pick back up where the dream woefully left off. But I have never been the type to fall back asleep once I'm woken up. It's annoying, but that little bird has ruined any chances of my having that dream again this morning. So instead I slide my hand down inside of my panties and begin to touch myself. If the two faceless men in my dream can't get me off, I'll just have to do it on my own. I massage tiny, soft circles into my clit, rolling my hips slowly as I cling to the sensory memory of two men touching me at once, four rough hands caressing my body and bringing me pleasure. Sure, maybe it's a little odd to be doing this here, in my childhood bedroom. But then again, it's not like I didn't touch myself in this same bed as a horny teenager years ago. I begin to rub faster and harder, my mouth falling open as my breaths come more quickly. I arch my back, giving in to the waves of bliss rippling through my body, and cum with a shuddering sigh.

I lie there for a few minutes, coming down from the high. As my pleasure ebbs away, my stress comes rushing back in to take its place. I groan and crawl out of bed, my toes curling when they touch the cool wooden floors. I trudge out of the bedroom, still decorated as it was when I lived here four years ago, before I headed off to university in New York. I walk down the quiet hallway, the walls lined with family portraits and terrible paintings I made as a kid. I don't know why my parents held on to all this stuff, but it's also impossible for me to imagine this house any other way. The organized clutter, the personal touches, even the flaws-- they all make me feel at home. This is a house of love, full of happy memories that I cherish above all else.

Which is why, I think to myself as I get into the

shower, I have to find a way to keep the house. This place is my heart and soul, and I can't bear to let it go. In fact, this house is basically the whole reason I moved back home from New York. I went off to college in Syracuse, getting my master's degree in creative writing. It was a great experience, and at the end of it, I landed a well-known agent in the city. She wanted me to move to Brooklyn and write there, so she was a little put out when I moved back here to North Carolina.

But the truth is, as much as I loved it up north, nowhere in the world inspires me quite like home does. This house lies in the picturesque foothills of the Blue Ridge Mountains, shaded by huge trees. Hiking trails leading to gorgeous waterfalls or cliffs with breathtaking views riddle these hills. My family home is on the edge of a forest, safely secluded from the suburbs and the hustle and bustle of Asheville. Growing up here was idyllic: playing in the woods from dawn till dusk, fishing in the creeks, climbing trees, picking wild strawberries and foraging for mushrooms with my pseudo-hippie parents. This old house has stood proudly on the hill surrounded by trees since the early 1900s, long before my parents bought the house and fixed it up. They got it for cheap back in the '80s, since it was a falling-apart old Victorian relic at the time. But they refurbished and renovated everything, breathing new life into the old beauty.

I assumed my parents would live here forever, but when I went off to college, they decided to retire to Florida. They want those white sandy beaches and a change of scenery, so they left the house to me. So I moved home, planning to use this place as a writer's retreat, to inspire my work. But then my mother fell ill. Suddenly, the only way they could keep to their retirement plan was to sell off everything. The house is our final asset. And now it's up for grabs, too, because some realty development company flashed a big number at my parents. An offer they could not afford to refuse. My mom required an emergency surgery, and it was an expensive one. The months of rehabilitation were pricey, too, even with their great insurance. Suddenly, our comfortable lives were turned upside down. She's been getting treated down in Florida, close to the beachside cottage they're renting for cheap.

Thankfully, my mother recovered from her illness, no doubt soothed and nursed back to health by a combination of my father's devotion and the balmy sea air. But this still leaves our family home hanging in the balance. I've spent the last few weeks struggling to figure out how I can scrounge up money to save the house. As a freelance writer with a kickass agent, I make fairly good money. And since moving back here, my writing has flourished. I love to write romance novels, often centered around a cozy small town where everyone knows each other. Living here in the beautiful countryside is exactly the right location for that kind of writing. My success is slowly building, and I live comfortably. But it's still not enough money to match the massive amount these developers are offering. I've tried fundraising. I've considered taking out loans... but nothing seems to be a good plan.

I dry off and get dressed, then walk outside into the brisk autumn air to check the mail. The leaves on the trees are turning vivid shades of orange and gold, like a blazing fire through the forest. It's beautiful. I'll never get tired of seeing the leaves turn. I just hope I can find a way to hold onto this place, whatever it takes.

I reach into the mailbox and pull out a letter with my parents' name on it. I open up the envelope and read it over, noting the header at the top that says WILSON & WARREN DEVELOPMENT COMPANY. The letter informs my parents that an inspector will be coming by soon to appraise the house and see how to go about demolishing it.

"Wait. What?" I murmur, my heart racing. I read over it again, just to be sure.

"Demolishing the house?" I gasp, feeling rage build up inside me. I thought they were just buying it to sell, not to destroy it! This place, with all its memories and history, knocked down into rubble… I won't stand for it. I storm back into the house and yank my long reddish-blonde hair back into a pony-tail, pull on a sweater over my tank top and jeans, put on my boots, and head out to my car. I look up the address for the realty office online, punch it into my GPS, and get on the road. I'm fuming, my heart pounding so fast I feel like I might be sick. I am not about to let these bastards destroy my house!

I'm amazed that I don't get stopped by the police for speeding so much, but it seems like luck is on my side for the moment. I hit almost entirely green lights as I rocket into town, leaving the woods behind. I pull up to a historic-looking old building with a brand new sign that reads WILSON & WARREN in large gold lettering. This is the place.

I hop out of the car and march straight into the office, where a petite brunette is sitting behind a receptionist desk. She looks up to smile at me, but her smile fades when she sees the undoubtedly scary look on my face. "C-Can I help you, miss?" she says nervously.

"Yeah," I answer, going straight up to the desk and leaning forward. "You can tell me where I can find Wilson or Warren or whoever is the guy trying to destroy my house."

"Oh. Um, ma'am, I'm sorry to tell you this, but Mr. Wilson and Mr. Warren have very full schedules. They have meetings booked up all day. All month, actually," she says meekly.

"I don't care. I demand to speak to whoever's in charge here," I say, folding my arms over my chest defiantly. "In fact, I'm not leaving until I get that meeting."

The receptionist looks petrified. "I-I understand you're upset, but there really isn't anything I can do to help you except make an appointment for you to meet with someone, perhaps next month?" she offers, wincing already in anticipating of my anger.

I hate being like this. I'm not usually the type to cause drama, and I know I shouldn't direct my anger at her. It's not her fault. But I have to stand my ground.

"Next month won't cut it. I need to speak to somebody now," I tell her firmly.

I hear the click and creak of a door opening down the hall and then heavy footsteps. A tall, impossibly handsome man with dark hair and dark eyes, a square jaw, and broad shoulders comes walking up to stand beside the desk. He's looking at me quizzically, but with a faint hint of amusement on his face that makes me even angrier.

"What seems to be the problem?" he asks coolly.

"You are!" I shoot back. "You and your partner are trying to tear down my house, and I will not stand for it. That house is a piece of history. It's an antique beauty. It's the most amazing house in the world and I will not let you destroy it."

He nods slowly, taking in my words. Then he gives me an affable smile. "Okay. My partner and I will meet with you. But it'll have to be after business hours because, as Janet here informed you, we have very busy schedules. What do you say we meet at the Blue Ridge Grille around seven o'clock tonight?" he offers.

I have half a mind to keep shouting, but I force myself to be calm. "Yes. Okay. Sure. We'll do that then. Seven PM at the Grille. I'll see you there," I tell him. I turn tail and march out of there, get back into my car, and drive home, wondering what the hell I'm going to say tonight that could possibly change their minds.

~

*I*t's seven o'clock, and I'm sitting in my car, in the parking lot outside the Blue Ridge Grille, trying not to have a meltdown. I got here way too early in my eagerness to get this meeting over and done with. I wasn't sure what to wear, so I just put on a little black dress with black tights, black heels, and a cherry-red peacoat. Of course, it wasn't until arriving here that I realized my outfit is probably better suited for a first date than a meeting with the two evil men who are plotting to tear down my family home and wreck my dreams. I don't want them to think I'm trying to impress them even though, well, I guess I am trying to impress them. Anything to make them reconsider their plans.

Finally, I force myself to open the car door and get out. I take a deep breath and stride into the restaurant, looking around for the table. The maitre'd looks me up and down and says, "Emma? Is that you?"

I glance over distractedly to see a guy I went to

high school with. I give him a smile. It's always nice to see a familiar face. It's part of what I love about a small town. "Hi, Dave. It's good to see you. I'm looking for a table... might be under the name Wilson. Or Warren."

He points over at a corner booth, where two men are seated. "Just over there. Don't keep them waiting, we can catch up later," he says with a wink.

I hurry over to the table, trying not to feel sick with nervousness. Both men stand up when I approach, like true gentlemen. I'm stunned to see that both of them are jaw-droppingly hot. There's the man I met this morning, with his dark hair and brown eyes, and next to him is an equally sexy guy, with blond hair and green eyes.

The man with the dark hair extends a hand and says, "Hi. I'm Travis Wilson. This is my business partner, Jake Warren. And judging from our short conversation this morning, I have a feeling you must be Emma Reed."

I nod, looking back and forth between them. Suddenly I feel very vulnerable and... weirdly, annoyingly turned on. I have a feeling it has some-thing to do with my sexy dream last night. But I have to ignore that. It's business time.

"Yes. I'm Emma Reed," I tell them, taking a seat. "And I am here to beg you not to destroy my house."

"Cutting right to the chase, I see," says Warren. "I like that."

"She's very confident," adds his partner, both of them eyeing me approvingly.

I blush, half with shyness and half out of anger. "I need you to take me seriously, please. Look, that house is my heart and soul. I have so many wonderful memories there. It's been there since the turn of the last century and it would be a travesty to lose it. Not just for me but for the community. It's a beautiful house. And I don't know what your plans are, but--"

"Our plan is to tear it down, clear out the forest, and build a golf course," Warren interrupts. "It's a deal that will bring in millions, possibly billions, in revenue. Both for us and for the community. Tourism would skyrocket. Wealthy businessmen and playboys would choose this place over Boca Raton, Malibu."

"But--but--" I splutter, losing traction. "That's not what we're known for. We already have tourists here every year to hike and fish and enjoy nature as it is. We like the peace and quiet. A golf course would just be... unnatural."

"Unnatural?" Wilson asks, raising an eyebrow. "So this is an ecological issue?"

"No. Yes. Well, partly. But mainly I am here to ask you-- beg you-- to please just let my house remain. I know my parents owe money, but I'm doing my best to help them pay it off. This house is the last thing we have left. Please don't take it from us. Please," I ask them passionately.

Both men exchange looks of smug curiosity, which makes me nervous.

"You would do anything, yes?" asks Warren.

"Yes. Anything," I answer firmly. Wilson rummages through his briefcase on the seat beside him and slides a document across the table to me. Frowning in confusion, I read it over. My eyes widen and my heart pounds wildly. I look at both men in shock.

"What is this?" I ask quietly.

"A contract," Wilson says coolly.

"Yes, I see that. But... what you're asking of me... This is crazy," I admit, putting the paper back down. "I-I can't possibly do that. It's wrong."

"How so? You want to save your house, and we want a willing participant for an evening of enjoyment," Warren explains, as though it's the simplest thing in the world. "As soon as Travis told me about your outburst this morning, about how passionate and gorgeous you were, I drew up this contract. I'm a businessman. I'm pragmatic. And the way I see it, this is a win-win."

I lean in closely and whisper, "Are you sure? This seems, I don't know, illegal or something. Besides, how do I know I can trust you?"

Wilson grins. "I suppose you don't. But you said you would try anything."

I bite my lip, thinking it over. These men want to fuck me. Tonight. No holds barred. And in exchange, I might just save the family home. I flash back to my sexy dream from last night. In a way, tonight could actually be a dream come true.

"Okay," I tell them. "Let's do it, then."

Wilson glances at the watch on his wrist. "The evening begins... now." Both men stand up and gesture for me to follow. I guess dinner isn't actually happening. They want to get started immediately. They leave a hundred-dollar bill on the table and we all head out of the restaurant to the confusion of the maitre'd.

"So, should I drive to meet you somewhere else or...?" I ask.

Wilson opens the door of a shiny black Cadillac. "No. We'll take my car."

Warren gets into the back seat and I reluctantly follow, not knowing what the hell they have in store for me. "You know, my mom used to tell me never to get into a car with a stranger," I tell them as Wilson gets behind the wheel and drives us away from the restaurant in the direction of my house.

"After tonight, we won't be strangers anymore," Warren says. "We intend to get to know you very, very well."

And with that, he leans in and kisses me. I freeze up at first, not expecting him to move so quickly. But he caresses my face with one hand, the other trailing down to grope my breasts through my dress, and I moan. Wilson glances back at us in the rear view mirror, watching as Warren feels me up. My body is warming to his touch, leaning into him as his hands slide up and down, grabbing my ass, my breasts, my hips. They are both impeccably dressed, with the kind of cologne that smells intoxicatingly delicious. Warren hoists me onto his lap, yanking up my dress so I can straddle him while we kiss. At first I was worried, but now, I think I might actually enjoy it. He smacks my ass and begins kissing my neck, nipping and sucking, leaving purplish bruises in his wake. I moan and close my eyes, giving in to the intense sensations.

Before it can go any further, I mumble, "I'm a virgin."

Wilson chuckles in the front seat. "We know. I could tell just by looking at you. But don't worry, we intend to take very good care of you tonight, Emma."

Warren slides his hand down between us, his fingertips stroking my clit through the thin fabric of my tights. I shiver and moan, giving in to the sensations. He kisses my neck and plays with my nipples while his other hand works my clit. All the while I can feel his massive, rock-hard cock straining against my thigh. I've never had a cock inside me before, but I'm nearly salivating for it. Warren strokes my clit faster and faster, rocking against me, until I'm cumming, making my tights all wet.

"Oh my god," I gasp.

"Good girl," Warren whispers, kissing me. He unzips his pants and pulls out his enormous shaft, placing it in my hand. I swallow nervously as I start to stroke his immense length, hoping I do it right. By the look on his face, I'm doing just fine. He groans and pushes up into me as I pump his hard rod with both hands. I want him to feel as good as I do. This carries on for a few minutes, until Travis clears his throat.

"I think it's time to switch off for a minute, don't you?" he says pointedly. Warren chuckles and nods.

"Get up there and suck his cock," Warren commands me. Wordlessly, I climb up into the passenger seat, thankful that there's nobody around on these dark country roads. Wilson unbuttons his slacks and slides his cock out. His is massive, too, seemingly too big for my mouth. I give him a worried look but he only smiles.

"You can handle it, Emma," he says. "Go ahead. Suck my cock. Right here in the open."

I crawl over and crouch down, lowering my head into his lap and letting my tongue flick lightly over the engorged head of his shaft. "That's it, baby. Keep going," he urges me.

I slowly pull his full length into my mouth, my cheeks aching as his enormous thickness stretches my mouth. "Oh, fuck yes. Just like that," Wilson groans, pressing gently on my head. As nervous as I am, it turns me on to know that he likes it. I begin to bob up and down on his cock, relaxing my jaw to take him in down to the hilt, the head of his cock brushing against the back of my throat. To my surprise, I don't gag or cough at all.

"No gag reflex, huh?" Wilson growls. "We can make use of that."

He pushes my head down a little harder and I suck him off eagerly, pleased to be doing a good job. I deepthroat him again and again, feeling my pussy dripping wet between my legs. At this rate, I can hardly wait to get to our destination. I need more. Finally, we arrive at my house. Wilson and Warren zip themselves back up and then Warren scoops me up over his shoulder to carry me up to the front door, making me giggle excitedly. I unlock the door and we burst into the house, both men feeling me up and kissing me all over. I'm almost overwhelmed with the pleasure of having two men pay so much attention to my virgin body. I've never been touched like this before. Wilson picks me up and they hurriedly carry me upstairs, walking into my bedroom and tossing me on the bed. Between the two of them, they get my clothes off in no time, leaving me naked and exposed in front of them. The men strip down, as well, and I finally get to see them naked in the light of my bedside lamp.

Both of them are muscular and powerfully built, with abdominal muscles that could cut glass, and arms that could throw me around like I weigh nothing. They stand over me, and immediately I remember my dream. Only this time, I can see their faces. This time, the men of my dreams are real.

Warren climbs onto the bed and lowers himself down to lick my slick pussy, working his finger inside of me while I squirm and writhe with pleasure. Meanwhile, Wilson takes two cords from his coat pocket on the floor and ties my wrists to the bed posts. It's exactly like my dream. I can hardly believe this is happening!

Wilson kisses me and fondles my bare breasts, rolling my nipples between his fingers and eliciting moans from me. "You've never been touched like this, have you?" he growls.

"Never," I answer breathlessly.

"Good," he says. "We want to break you in."

Warren pushes a second finger inside of me, hooking his fingers so that he strokes against that sensitive spot deep within that makes me whimper and sigh with pleasure. Wilson stands up on the bed, bracing himself against the wall, and pushes his cock into my mouth. I suck him off while Wilson fingers my cunny, and the stimulation pushes me over the edge. My pussy convulses and cums all over Warren's hand.

"Fuck yes," he snarls. "So nice and wet for me, baby. But you need something bigger than my two fingers, don't you?"

"Yes," I moan earnestly. "Please."

Wilson shoves his cock back in my mouth just as Warren slides his massive cock into my slick pussy. I tremble and whimper at the mingled pain and pleasure. He wastes no time in fucking me, pounding into my virginal hole so hard that I'm seeing stars. Meanwhile, Wilson doesn't let up either, fucking my throat until I can hardly breathe.

"You love this, don't you? Two cocks inside you," Warren hisses through gritted teeth.

"Feels good, doesn't it?" Wilson groans as he pounds into my throat. Tears are burning my eyes from the overwhelming pleasure. Warren's cock beats against my g-spot again and again, until finally I'm shuddering and screaming with another climax.

Wilson pulls his cock out of my mouth and gets off the bed, untying my wrists so I can move a little more while Warren fucks me hard. "I love the way your sweet little cunt feels, gushing honey all over my cock," he says, his voice low and rasping. "I'm going to make you cum again, Emma."

He reaches down to rub my clit while he slams into me, sending me into gasps and mewls of pleasure. I'm so overwhelmed I can barely stand it. Wilson watches, stroking himself, waiting for his turn to fuck the virgin. Warren picks me up and carries me over to the desk in the corner of my room, laying me back and pounding into me with my legs hooked over his shoulders.

"I'm--I'm not on birth control," I gasp.

"I don't care," he replies, and that only turns me on more. Somehow, the chance that he could put a baby inside me makes it hotter. The riskiness, the pure animalistic need these men have to pound into my cunny and pump me full of their hot, sweet cum. I'm ravenous for it. I can't wait to feel them fill me up.

"You want two cocks again?" Wilson growls in my ear.

I nod vigorously. "Oh god, yes."

Warren carries me back to the bed and lies down, picking me up like I weigh nothing at all and turning me to face away from him as I ride him, rolling my hips and bouncing up and down on his hard shaft. Wilson comes back over and stands in front of me. I tug his cock into my mouth and suck him hard, moaning with pleasure as Warren grabs my hips and thrusts up into me from below. He fucks me harder and faster, and I can feel him losing control.

"Fuck yes. Just like that," he groans, reaching up to smack my ass. I whimper in delicious pain, riding him faster, feeling his cock strike against my g-spot while he loses himself. I'm bobbing up and down on

Wilson's dick, nearly gagging myself in my need to fill myself up. I love the sensation of my mouth and pussy stuffed full with cock. I never want it to end.

But when Warren grabs hold of me and shoots his hot, sticky cum deep inside me, I realize how amazing that feels, too. I moan around Wilson's cock, squeezing my pussy to eke out every last drop of Warren's cum. When he's done with me, he gets up off the bed and Wilson pushes me down onto my knees, grabbing a handful of my hair as he shoves his cock into my dripping cunt before I can even react. He fucks me hard from behind, his balls slapping against my ass as he yanks my head back slightly. I feel so used, so fucked out of my mind, and I love it.

"Cum inside me," I whisper. "Please. Fill me up. Fuck that little pussy."

I've never said words like this out loud before, but Wilson seems to appreciate it. "Oh, you like that, hmm? A huge fucking cock shoved inside your sweet little cunt? Gonna pump you full of my cum, Emma," he purrs.

"Yes, yes, yes," I murmur. Just as he picks up the pace and slams into me again, I'm cumming with a cry of intense pleasure. "Fuck!" I cry out, tears in my eyes from bliss.

Wilson fucks me harder, slapping my ass so hard

that I know it'll leave a mark. Finally, after a few more sharp thrusts, he cums inside of me, pumping my cunny full of his seed. When he pulls out, I can feel both men's cum dripping down my thighs to stain my childhood bed. It feels so dirty, so wrong, and yet I don't feel bad at all. In fact, I feel better than I ever have before. Wilson scoops me up in his arms and the three of us head down the hall to shower off together, warm and cozy and exhausted.

As I stand there between them in the stream of hot, cleansing water, I ask meekly, "So? Do we have a deal?"

Both men chuckle, and then Warren says, "We have a deal."

~

I'm sitting on the front porch, watching as Jake mows the lawn and Travis carries in groceries from the car. I have my hand resting on my pregnant belly, a laptop next to me on the coffee table. In my lap is a letter from my editor, thanking me for my last manuscript, raving about how fantastic it was. Travis comes up the steps and leans down to kiss me on the lips, caressing my cheek. I smile up at him happily.

"What's that?" he asks, pointing to the letter.

"Just notes from the editor," I answer. "She loved my story."

"Well, of course she did. You're an amazing writer, sweetheart. I hope the baby gets some of your creativity," he says with a wink. "So, what sounds good for dinner tonight? Jake was talking about making his famous mac and cheese, but I was thinking maybe Italian."

"Oh god. Right now, both of those options sound amazing," I groan, patting my belly. I'm seven months pregnant, and just about any food is a welcome food in my book.

Jake comes up to us, wiping the sweat off his brow. He's shirtless, in his jeans and boots, looking every bit the sweaty, sexy handyman he's turned into since we all moved back into my house together. There have been lots of little things to fix here and there, and both my men have been amazing at helping keep the place tidy and functional while I'm wrapped up in being pregnant and a bestselling author at the same time.

"So, how's that mac and cheese sound?" Jake asks, beaming at us both.

"Or Italian takeout?" suggests Travis.

I bite my lip and think about it, then answer, "Hmm. Both," with a smile.

Travis laughs and nods. Both of my guys will do just about anything for me these days. He says, leaning down to kiss me, "That works for us. Why choose when you can have both?"

STEALING HER

"*A*nything to keep your job, Emily?"

Max Armstrong, CEO of the company I work for, throws my words back in my face with a tone dripping with hunger. He stands up from his desk and walks toward me, all six and a half feet of him looking even taller the closer he gets.

I bite my lip and take a lock of my dark hair in my hand to play with nervously. Why did I say that?

I was at least a head shorter than Max, with straight black hair that hung past my shoulders, pale skin, full lips, an upturned nose, and soft brown eyes that were sparkling with nervousness. I wore a blouse and pencil skirt that showed a little more of my long legs than I needed to. My perfume made me smell like lavender--work was stressful, so it was a scent I liked to keep around. My heels made me a lot taller than I was, but Max still dwarfed me.

He was an intimidating guy on a normal day.

But this isn't a normal day.

I'm standing in his office because he caught me stealing company money.

It wasn't much, considering how much the company rakes in. I should know, I'm one of the girl working the books. I thought a little change here and there wouldn't go missing--I have bills that need paying, after all.

Too bad Max Armstrong is a *very* hands-on CEO. He personally noticed the discrepancies in the books and called me into his office.

And now, he's ravishing me with his eyes.

"Anything at all?" he repeats, slowly pacing around me. I swallow.

"Yes, sir," I say softly.

"I like the way you say that," his deep, husky voice rumbles. "Did you know, before all this, your CV was on my desk for a promotion? You've caught my eye, Miss Andrews. I would have liked having you as my personal assistant."

What?!

"I did a little investigating in your internet use while I was at it," he says, and my face goes cherry-red. "Pornography at work, Emily? Really? I expect that from the men, but..."

"Please, Mr. Armstrong," I gasp, turning around and putting my hands on his chest, and I almost jump back as I realize just how rock-hard those pecs are. My instinct is to run my hands further down, but I take them back as if burned by fire. "I-I mean..."

He smiles and touches my chin with his finger and thumb, lifting my gaze back up to him. "It's okay, Emily," he says in a deep, reassuring voice. "We all have desires like that. It's what makes us human."

He brings his other hand around to my ass and pinches it.

I yelp, and my eyes go wide. Is he really doing this?! What would HR think? But I know that wouldn't matter. I'm a thief, and he's going to punish me any way he wants.

And if I'm honest with myself...something inside me wants to be punished.

"I've seen your pay, Emily," he growls as he pulls me closer to him, and my stomach bumps against his groin. I feel his rock-hard shaft under that tailored suit, and I realize he's hard for *me*. I never thought someone like him would want me, but the way he's looking at me is downright lustful. "You don't need the money. You weren't even stealing much. Why would a nice girl like you do something silly like this?"

"I…" I breathe, words lost.

I nearly jump out of my skin when a third voice speaks.

"Could it be that she just wanted to act out for attention?"

The voice comes from the CFO of the company, Taylor Barr. Where Max has short, black hair, Taylor has medium-length dark auburn hair that I've always wanted to run my hands through. I didn't even notice him entering the room.

"Ah, Taylor, you're here," Max remarks without looking away from me or moving his hand from my ass. "Good."

"What are you two doing?" I ask with short breaths.

"I found something very interesting in your porn history, Emily," Max says, and when I realize what he's talking about, I feel so petrified that I want to shrink away into nothing and be as far away as possible. "A menage fetish isn't something I expected from you. But you have good taste, at least."

"I'm sorry, Mr. Armstrong, I shouldn't have-"

"Please," he says, "call me Max. And Mr. Barr is

Taylor. We should get a little comfortable with each other if you'd like to hear us out."

My eyes go wide. They...they can't *possibly* be suggesting what I think they are.

"Max and I were talking about some of our *shared interests*," Taylor says as he approaches me from behind, and I feel his strong hands on my shoulders. He starts massaging my back and neck slowly. I'm so tense that it actually feels pretty incredible, but I'm too nervous to show it.

"We were going to hire a professional to cater to some of our unusual tastes," Max says, nodding down at me. "But your situation gave us an idea."

"One night," Taylor says. Max takes his hand off my ass, and Taylor holds my hips to pull my ass into his crotch. When I feel his hardness too, I know exactly what these two huge men are getting at. "One night where anything goes. You, me, and Max. We all make our dreams come true, and we can forget this little incident."

I don't know what to say. My heart is pounding, and my pussy is getting warm at just the thought of that. But this is so...just so wrong that I don't even know where to begin.

But if it's so wrong, why am I excited?

I look both of them in the eye, biting my lip.

"Well, Emily?" Max asks, casually squeezing my breasts as if I'm just another piece of his property. "What'll it be?"

～

I cannot believe myself.

My eyes are blindfolded, and that's the only piece of clothing on my entire body.

I'm kneeling on the conference table in the very room where Max and Taylor interviewed me for this job a year ago. I remember them sitting there and drinking me in with their eyes, but I never thought that would lead to this.

The smooth wood is cool on my knees and feet. My arms are behind my back, held together by soft yet strong handcuffs.

This is all part of the contract I signed to make this happen. The second my pen touched that paper, I knew I was in way over my head.

It's cool in the room, and my nipples are so stiff they feel hard. My makeup is perfect, but I'm not going to be able to see it until one of them decides to take the blindfold off.

Just when I'm starting to wonder if they're even coming or if this was some elaborate joke to humiliate me before firing me, the door swings open.

"Fuck," I hear Taylor groan, laden with desire, and I know he's talking about me. "She looks better than I could have hoped for."

"I was having second thoughts about this deal," I hear Max say, "but Emily, as always, you exceed expectations."

"Thank you, sirs," I say, barely above a squeak.

I smell their cologne as they get close to me, and their heavy footsteps move around the table like sharks circling prey.

That's all I am to them right now.

This is just for a deal, Emily, I tell myself. *That's the only reason you're doing this.*

But I know I'm lying to myself.

I'm going to love every second of this.

The deal is just an excuse.

I hear the sound of something unzipping in front of me, and my heart skips a beat. I'm kneeling right up next to the edge of the table, and I have no idea which of the men is in front of me.

"Let's start with something simple," I hear Max's voice in front of me. My heart flutters again. I don't know why, but I hoped he would be the one I get to taste first. The sound of fabric tells me he's pushing his underwear down, and suddenly, I feel something warm, soft, and firm gently slap me on the cheek.

It's his cock, and it's so much bigger than I expected it ever could have been.

I feel a strong, firm hand in my hair. His fingers run through my raven locks and squeeze into a gentle fist for a few moments before relaxing, but he doesn't let go.

"I'm a very hands-on CEO," he says. "You should know that by now if you've been paying attention, and I know you have. You might find me to be a bit...controlling."

As he says that, he forcibly turns my head to the left, and I feel the crown of his cock touch my soft lips. My face is red as a rose. This is tapping into my deepest, darkest desires. Everything about it is wrong, but my body wants it so badly that just waiting for them got me wet.

"Let's get started, shall we?" Max commands me, and I softly nod my head, feeling his warm cock grace my lips.

I open my mouth and let my tongue out.

My lips hold the bulging crown in place while I lick the opening of his cock, and I hear him draw in a sharp breath. With my eyes blinded, I feel all my other senses just a little bit more intensely, and having my hands behind my back really makes me helpless before them. I don't even know where Taylor is.

What I didn't tell them is that I'm a virgin. Everything I'm going on is pure instinct. I hope it serves me well, because my job depends on it.

My tongue starts at the base of his bulging cock, where I feel the crown's ridge meeting, and I move my tongue around at that soft base. I never thought my first time would be like this, but it sends ripples of excitement through my body.

I feel out the underside of his cock before I let my tongue go up his slit again, and this time, I feel him give a subtle but powerful pulse. It's faint, but it promises so, so much power in the cock behind it. I don't even know how long it is--but I'm going to find out soon.

I open my mouth a little more and take the whole crown of his cock into my mouth like a lollipop. And just like something sweet and delicious, I start turning my head and moving my tongue all over it. I let out a soft moan as I run my tongue around the whole girth of the crown.

I've seen cocks in porn before. I know how big they can get. But the sheer size of Max's crown promises something bigger than I've ever imagined.

His cock gets even stiffer as I play with his crown, and soon, I want more in me. I push myself forward, but Max pulls his hips back a little and holds my head in both hands.

"Oh no, you need to work for it, little miss," he says. That subtle command makes me shiver, and I want to work that much harder for him.

I start running my tongue up and down his slit in a steady rhythm. Up and down, up and down, feeling him pulse every few seconds as I start to get him more and more excited. He's such a big, powerful man, and his every move shows me how much control he has over me. That just makes me more excited to be able to get this kind of reaction from his cock.

After a few strokes at that pace, I move my tongue in a circle around his crown, then go back to massaging his slit. He seems to like that, and he rewards me by stroking my hair slowly with one hand while the other holds me firm.

"That's it," he groans, "good girl."

Those words get me even wetter, and I let out a moan of pleading.

"When Taylor and I interviewed you," Max says, "we talked about a little something in this very room, on this very table."

I got bolder with my tongue, and I slid it further under his cock than I ever had before. He lets me, and I realize I can take a little more of his shaft into me.

"We had this idea of a more interactive interview than you might be used to," Taylor's voice comes from behind me, and suddenly, I feel something heavy climbing up on the table.

It's Taylor himself.

He makes his way to my ass on his knees, and just as Max lets me take half of his whole cock into my mouth, I feel Taylor grab my ass with both hands.

"I think our idea is going to work out just fine," Taylor groans.

While he unzips, I start exploring Max's shaft with my tongue in every way I possibly can. I feel its weight on my tongue--and it's only halfway in, if my estimate is right. It's heavy, girthy, and full of need. I push it against the roof of my mouth and start massaging the soft underside gently, and on every fifth stroke, I bring my tongue back up to tease his slit.

"She's damn good at this," Max muses in a thick, husky tone.

"Oh yeah?" Taylor says. "Let's see if that checks out back here."

I feel Taylor's cock perch on my pussy lips as if waiting at a gate, and my whole body shivers with excitement. The second I took Max's cock into my mouth, I knew I wanted something to match it between my legs.

Taylor's manhood is all I could have wanted and more.

"I've thought about this a lot more than you realize, Emily," Taylor says as he rubs his rough hands over my asscheeks. "Did you know that? Some nights, when I just can't get to sleep, I hit the shower and think of you while I get my release. But I have a feeling the real thing is going to be better than I ever imagined."

Something deep and primal in me feels absolutely excited by everything he says, and on instinct, I arch my back and push my ass back onto him.

He isn't taken by surprise for a second.

He pushes his cock into me as soon as I start pushing back on him, and just like Max's crown went into my mouth, Taylor's goes into my slick, wet pussy.

The feeling is unbelievable.

It's fulfilling and warming all at the same time, but it's just as terrifying as it is exciting--his cock is *huge*, and I honestly have no idea if it will fit.

"Fuck, you're tight," he growls, and he squeezes my ass as he works his way a little further in. "How does that feel, Emily?"

I moan a deep, loving reply, and I hear a chuckle from him. The next second, I feel a sharp slap on my ass, and my whole body jolts.

"We're not even started yet."

Max's cock throbs in my mouth, and as I take more of it closer to my throat, Taylor sinks deeper-- much deeper than I was expecting. I let out a whimpering sigh of delight as I feel his thick cock grind against the front of my pussy, and as he does, he reaches around with one hand to start fingering my clit while he thrusts into me.

I give a long, sincere moan into Max's cock as I feel Taylor invading my pussy, both inside and out. I feel even more tightly restrained with two of my holes stuffed with cock, but I wouldn't want to be anywhere else in the world right now.

These two guys are filling me up in every possible way, and I love every second of it.

Taylor's pushing behind me starts thrusting me further onto Max's cock, and before I know it, I'm like a sleeve between the two of the. Max has his hands in my hair, stroking me and murmuring periodically with my steady rhythm. My tongue feels tired, but there is no way I'm slowing down, not now.

"Good girl," he mutters now and then, "just like that."

I don't know what it is about those two words, but they make me feel so whole and warm that it makes it all that much easier for Taylor to keep bucking into my pussy.

Taylor is lavishing me with attention. His fingers move in little circles on my clit, and he has a way of keeping his fingers from getting in the way of his cock that I don't understand. His long reach and massive cock make it all possible, and it's so delicious that I never want it to end.

Meanwhile, the way his cock is grinding against my insides at the same time is making me feel tighter by the second.

For some reason, the thought of cumming through all this never occurred to me. When I signed my contract, I thought I'd just be a toy for them.

But these guys have their hands all over me, and there's pure desire in their touch. They're here to make me feel happy as much as I'm here for them, and oh my god, it's working so much better than all the times I spent touching myself to this idea.

Taylor starts rocking back and forth in a steady

rhythm, just like I'm doing with Max's cock. Taylor's cock strokes my innermost depths, parts of me I never knew a man could touch, and all the while, that paired with his constant torture of my clit makes me feel like a wire that's getting wound back too tight.

I'm so close, and I just need to be plucked.

"You're so fucking wet," Taylor growls. "You've wanted this a long time, haven't you? Is this what you've been thinking about when you watch porn on company time, little miss Emily?"

"Mmhmm," I murmur through a mouth full of my boss's cock, and it makes Max's cock pulse harder than ever before.

Suddenly, I taste a drop of precum on my tongue, and I feel a vigor in me I didn't know I was capable of.

The guys have been pushing me back and forth between them this whole time, but their enthusiasm makes me start using my legs to help them with the rhythm. I arch my back every time Taylor thrusts, and I feel his cock pulsing and twitching in response to me.

And finally, I start clenching my pussy around his cock to feel the full pressure of his thrusts in me, and I spill over the edge.

I give an urgent murmur through Max's cock, and they guys get the message--I'm about to come.

They get fiercer and fiercer. Max tightens his grip on my hair, and Taylor explores my body more fiercely than ever before with no end in sight. He grinds against my g-spot deep inside me while toying with my clit, and I feel my pussy tighten, a tightness that spreads up to my lower abdomen, and finally, with a burst of relief, warmth spreads out from there to my whole body.

"Ohhh, that's it," Taylor groans as I come all over his cock. "Let it all out, little miss Emily, we've got you."

This is supposed to be my punishment, and my restraints show that, but they're so comforting that if this is punishment, I want them to punish me forever.

My body shakes and writhes, but I try so hard to keep my poise. I want to be a good little ornament for them on the table for them to fuck, but I feel so wet that I don't know how I can keep myself from just falling over into a useless puddle.

"Hold on," Max says once my orgasm dies down. He gently pushes my head off his cock, and I let out a whimper of protest.

Have I done something wrong?

I let my tongue run along his cock until it's all the way out, and it leaves me with a wet pop. Taylor stops pumping, but I feel his cock pulsing with desire in me while he pinches my ass a little.

"Let's shake it up a little," I hear Max say. My blindfold is still on, but I can feel his breath as he gets close to me and holds my chin in his hand. "How would you like to have both of us in you at once, little miss Emily?"

"H-how…?" I ask, and I can almost *hear* Max's smile.

"With a little lube and some patience," Taylor answers, and I hear the sound of something plastic opening. I realize with a shiver that it's lube.

Max leans forward and kisses me on the mouth, and I feel his warmth on me while I hear Taylor squirting some of the lube onto his hand. The next second, I feel something in my ass.

I suck in a sharp breath as Taylor's finger enters by tight asshole and starts moving around in it.

I've never thought much about things going into my butt. I didn't realize it was something that was very fun for girls.

But the way Taylor is touching me, it feels like he has an understanding of my body that I could never approach.

He moves in a wide circle around in my ass, and his other hand keeps massaging my clit. "Just relax," he purrs in a deep husky tone. "Yeah, that's it. Nice and slow."

I lose track of time as Taylor readies my ass for him and Max kisses me. My heart is racing, and I'm both excited and nervous about what could come next.

Then, Taylor leaves my asshole, and I find myself wishing he were back, but I know something so much better is on its way.

Max lifts me up by my hips as if I weigh nothing. His strength is unbelievable.

"Just follow my lead," he says, and he walks my bare feet toward him until I hear his frame bump against the wall. "And remember that no matter what, I've got you."

I nod softly, breathing in shallow, hot breaths through my mouth.

Max lifts me up by my hips again, and this time, he perches my pussy on *his* cock.

Then, I feel Taylor's lubed-up cock grind between my asscheeks.

"Oh god," I gasp, scared.

"Do you still want this?" Max asks one more time.

"More than anything," I breathe, and as ashamed as I am...it's the truth.

Max lets me sink onto his cock.

I cry out in bliss as his whole shaft fills me up. I'm already trained for him from Taylor, but the pressure of my whole body held up by just his strength is unbelievable. He starts bouncing me up and down on his cock, using his arms to move me the whole time. He grinds against every part of me with that thick, veined shaft and bulging crown I nursed in my mouth just minutes ago.

While I get closer to another orgasm, Taylor massages his cock between my asscheeks, and I feel him pulsing and throbbing back there too.

Max is like a machine, and the steady, unstoppable rhythm makes that familiar tension well up in my body again. My hands are still cuffed behind my back. If Max didn't know what he was doing, this could end very painfully and awkwardly.

But Max is a master.

"I'm going to get you good and relaxed," Max murmurs into my ear. "And then the real fun can start." He kisses my lips and invades my mouth with his tongue. My stiff nipples brush against his broad, muscular chest, and I'm soon completely sandwiched between the men.

The combination of all of it makes me feel hot, safe, and overwhelmed with feeling at every possible part of my body. I start whimpering helplessly into his kiss, begging for more and more as he gets faster.

Soon, I can't help myself, and I feel my tension spiral out of control as I cum

The orgasm makes me shake, legs dangling, but the guys lean into me to keep me supported. Every part of my body relaxes with the orgasm, and just as I let out a ragged sigh to show that...Taylor enters me.

He starts slow, but I feel him at my asshole, first the tip, and it's so huge that I truly don't know whether it's all going to fit.

But he was liberal with the lube, and just like he said, he goes patiently. Max keeps moving me up and down on his shaft, and Taylor is stunningly good at keeping pace. Soon, half of his cock enters me.

The feeling is unlike any other.

Having a cock in you is amazing. But two cocks in two holes so close to each other doubles the intensity, and when Max breaks his kiss, I gasp so desperately that you'd think I've just been given water after nearly dying of thirst.

"God, give me more, please!" I beg. I need this. I

need this so badly I don't know how I went so long in my life without this.

Sweet, caring Taylor listens to my every word, and his dominant hands squeeze my ass as I relax as much as possible to let him in further.

Soon, the two guys are totally inside me, and they work together in perfect harmony to make me feel new, stunning heights.

"Emily, you're so much tighter now," Max shudders.

"You can forget about getting fired, little miss," Taylor teases me, taking my hair in his hand and pulling me back enough that he can kiss my neck. "I'm keeping you around as long as I want."

Those words bring me so close to the edge of another orgasm that it's painful, and this time, I can feel that the guys are right there too. They start pounding into me harder and harder. I don't know how they're this coordinated, but they've worked together for years, so their minds must just be incredible at staying in sync.

Inside me, I feel Max's cock thrust up the whole length of my pussy, and as he lifts me up, Taylor's cock goes up my ass. It massages everything inside me, and I feel like my loins are one big melting pot of feelings. Tears come to my eyes--tears of joy for what I'm feeling from head to toe.

Is this an orgasm about to happen, or have I been in one slow-burn orgasm for the past few minutes?

Time loses meaning. I'm just a mess on two cocks that can't get enough of me, and I could swear they're getting thicker by the second.

"I'm gonna cum in you, Emily. Do you want that?" Max growls.

"Yes, Max," I hear my voice saying. I don't know where it comes from--I didn't ask for a condom, and I don't want one. Something primal is awakened in me. "I want you both to fill me up. Every day I think about how fucking virile you both are. I want you to fill me with your fucking cum, and I want all of it!"

Their words have had so much power over me that it's almost surprising what kind of effect mine have on them. They start groaning and losing their natural rhythm, instead bucking up into me with abandon.

I feel my whole body tightening, and I'm a little afraid of it this time. This is something bigger and stronger than I've ever felt before, and it's not going to hold anything back.

Neither are they.

Our groans fill the room as we all get closer and

closer, their bodies rubbing against mine and sending electricity to every little part of me until...

I feel Taylor's cum shoot up into my ass first, and half a second later, Max's fills up my pussy. There's so much from both of them that I think something's wrong for a second, but no, I'm trapped between two of the most virile, potent men I've ever met who are both filling me up with their cum, and their ragged groans tell me that this is sweeter than anything they've felt before.

When I'm truly filled up in both holes, Max lifts me up and off both of them, but I feel more spurts of their thick, hot cum hitting my body. The reach is incredible--one of Max's shoots up and hits me on the chin, while one of Taylor's does the same and gets in my hair.

I'm a complete mess, and I've never felt better.

Soon, I melt back into Taylor's arms, listening to the groans from both the men over me. His hand pulls the blindfold off me, and I flutter my eyes to see the two men grinning down at me, their faces blushing and satisfied.

"That was...oh my god," I coo as Max uncuffs me and lets me snuggle into Taylor's arms. He stands me up, and I lean forward onto Max's chest and kiss his muscles while Taylor massages his cock with my ass.

"I think..." Max starts, breathing raggedly, "I think we might just need to revisit your position in the company, Miss Andrews."

"I think I'd like that," I say.

The worst day ever became the best, and all it took was a little embezzlement and a lot of lube.

~

Seven months later was the first time that Max and Taylor couldn't fit both of their cocks into me at the same time.

I was too swollen with my pregnancy by then.

When I told them they had knocked me up, we were all three ecstatic--and when they both proposed to me at the same time, I was over-whelmed. Money makes incredible things happen, though, and within a few weeks, the two guys had me living at their holiday house in the Bahamas.

I got to live out my pregnancy with the two of them working from 'home' there nearly every day, and if one absolutely had to be away for work, the other stayed behind to keep me company.

It was strange, being shared by two amazing guys. I got to know them more and realize just how well they worked together. There was no jealousy between them--all they cared about was me, and I was more than happy to fill that role while they filled me up.

Every night was something new. I took their cum in my mouth, ass, pussy, and every inch of my body over the months. The heavier I got with my pregnancy, the more enthusiastic they seemed.

We even roleplayed a few times, recreating that fateful day that brought us all together.

The only downside was that I wasn't allowed to handle the books anymore. Instead, they just gave me their credit cards and told me to go crazy. And no matter how much I thought I was spending, they always told me to push it further.

And this morning, as I wake up to the feeling of Max's tongue massaging my clit and Taylor's mouth on my swollen breasts, I feel like I've got a long time ahead of me to meet that challenge.

AWAKENING HER

J'm alone in the locker room, lying on the cold, hard metal bench next to my locker. I'm staring up at the ceiling, letting my hands roam up and down my body. I curl my fingers under the tight, cropped shirt I wear with the words MAPLETOWN TORNADOES emblazoned across in gold lettering.

I have a flouncy little skirt on, the kind that barely falls to mid-thigh, and knee-high socks with my athletic sneakers. I bite my lip, moaning as my hands slip over my full breasts, groping and rubbing my nipples until they're so stiff you can see them straining through the fabric of my top. My pompoms lie on the floor next to the bench, put aside for a moment of risky pleasure.

I cut out of practice a little early, claiming an ankle injury, just so I could sneak in here and have some alone time. I'm so fucking turned on and frustrated all the time. My roommate is always home, hogging the bathroom and keeping me awake all night studying with the light on.

I wish she was the kind of girl who went out partying, just so that I could get a night alone to myself for once. But no, just like every other classmate of mine, she's so focused and driven in her classwork. That's all anyone seems to care about around here: making good grades. It's like nobody knows how to have fun anymore.

So, I am making time for my own little bit of fun wherever I can. If that means touching myself in the girls' locker room, then so be it. Besides, I have to admit, I look sexy as hell in my tight little uniform.

I know for a fact that's why Coach Scott Robinson, the tall, handsome former football player who now coaches the team here, always stares at me during practice. He just can't seem to keep his eyes off of me, glancing over so often that I'm surprised the football players haven't noticed yet. But then again, football jocks are always so dumb.

I should know. My high school sweetheart was a football player. Captain of the team, in fact, and I liked him so much that I almost gave up my most precious gift to him: my virginity. But on the night I intended to offer him that precious gift, he dumped me. Out of nowhere. Just because we are attending two different colleges. He's only an hour away, but I guess that was just too far for him. I wasn't worth his time.

But whatever.

I'm so over guys my own age now. They're all so immature, irresponsible, inexperienced, and just flat-out not attractive to me anymore. I get hit on all the time on campus, but nobody, and I mean nobody, arouses my fantasies quite like older men.

In particular, two older men.

I moan, rubbing my clit through my damp panties, rolling my hips as I caress my full breasts. I imagine Coach Robinson walking in on me here, finding me spread-eagled and moaning like the little slut I am. What would he do, I wonder? For the sake of my fantasy, I like to imagine that he would find me sexy.

Irresistible.

He's got to be at least six-foot-four, and I'm barely over five feet tall, and incredibly petite. I have to be, since I'm the girl at the top of the pyramid. I'm the girl getting tossed into the air to do flips. I'm the leader of the pack, and I'm good at what I do. Good enough, in fact, to get a full ride to Mapletown College on a cheerleading scholarship. That also sets me apart from my classmates, who are all here to study and become scientists, professors, doctors, all those boring careers that brainy people do.

I'm only here because of my body. The way I can move it, entice my audience, almost seducing them into cheering for my team. It's almost as though every shake of my ass and swing of my hips begs the question: "Don't you want to pull for the winning team?"

And in my experience, I'm always pulling for the winning team. Even here, at college, our football team is renowned in the region for being unbeatable. Unstoppable. And a lot of that is due to the expert strategies and tactical know-how of Coach Robinson.

He's a genius on the sidelines. He knows exactly what it's like to be on that football field, since he's a former player. And he still looks the part. He's probably in his mid thirties, but he's way hotter than any of the guys he coaches.

I can just picture him walking up to me, his cock hard and erect, straining against the fabric of those tight jeans. He would look down at me with lust in those stormy gray eyes. I imagine what it would feel like to fuck him. It's hard to imagine, since I'm a virgin. But I can try. I bet it would feel a million times better than touching myself.

I rub tight little circles around my clit, moaning and gasping as I imagine him picking me up and putting me on his lap. I can almost feel the way his huge, rough hands would slide down my body, groping my tits, grabbing my ass. He would rut up against my cunt with that big, meaty dick, both of us getting off on the friction. Just as I'm about to cum, I hear the clatter of footsteps approaching.

The team must be finished with practice. I can't get caught like this!

I hop up and race into the locker room showers, jumping into a stall and quickly stripping off my uniform. I drape it up over the wall and turn on the water, my heart pounding as the girls trickle into the locker room, chatting and giggling among themselves.

Now totally naked in the steamy shower stall, I lean back against the wall and touch myself with no fabric in the way. I circle my clit again and again, reveling in the riskiness of what I'm doing. My teammates are just on the other side of that thin curtain, talking to each other and gossiping. I almost let a moan of pleasure slip out, and I clap my hand over my mouth while my other hand strokes my clit faster and harder. The danger of getting caught, of someone watching me touch myself doesn't scare me like it should. I realize with surprise that it actually just turns me on even more. I rock my hips, sighing with bliss, now imagining the other target of my affections: Professor Will Byron.

He's my English professor, the older man of my dreams. He's tall and handsome, with kind brown eyes the color of warm cinnamon and a smile that could melt the panties off of any woman. He has salt-and-pepper hair, and he's always wearing those sexy button-up white shirts with the sleeves rolled to his elbows, showing off his strong forearms. I just know there's a sexy body underneath those clothes. I imagine him finding me here in the shower. Joining me. Wrapping those big arms around me and kissing me while he fingers my tight little cunny...

"Ohh!" I moan, gushing cum all over my fingers. The girls talking on the other side of the curtain stop for a moment and I hastily add, "Stubbed my toe! Ow!"

This seems to be enough to fool them. They go back to chatting as though nothing happened, and I smile to myself, knowing the truth. Damn, it's hot to think that I could have gotten caught at any moment.

I wait around long enough for all my teammates to shower off and get dressed, then head out for the afternoon. When the coast is clear, I towel off and put my uniform back on, a dangerously tempting idea planting itself in my mind. I am so sexually frustrated that I've resorted to touching myself in the girls' locker room. It's not enough for me anymore. I need something better. Something real. *Someone* real.

Normally, I would put on my street clothes after practice, but this afternoon I have another plan in mind. A plan that requires this cheerleading uniform. I walk up to the foggy mirrors and touch up my curly blonde pigtails, making sure my makeup isn't smeared from my steamy shower session. Once I'm satisfied with my appearance, I grab my duffel bag and head out, grinning to myself about my plan. I know it's a crazy idea, but I also know that college is the time to experiment. To mess around. Make questionable decisions. After all, I'm eighteen now. I'm definitely old enough to make my own choices, even if they may seem like crazy choices to someone else. I have to jump on this plan before I get the chance to talk myself out of it. I have momentum right now, and giving myself an orgasm hasn't slaked my thirst in the least. In fact, now I'm thirsty for more. And I know exactly where to look for it.

I check my phone and bite my lip, nervously sliding the screen open to see if I have any new text messages. My heart skips a beat when I see that I have a message from my favorite Professor. Will Byron. The text reads: *I'm here in my office. Feel free to come by.*

"Don't mind if I do," I murmur to myself giddily.

I text back: *I'm cumming. See u soon.*

I giggle, hoping that my innuendo sticks. It should. After all, Professor Byron is kind of the king of innuendo. He's been teaching us a segment on erotic literature throughout the ages this semester, and he doesn't back down from even the raunchiest historical texts. Hell, lately we've even been studying contemporary romance novels in class! I've never had such a cool, relaxed teacher before. And I have definitely never had a teacher that sexy.

Plus. he's a total sweetheart. I first went to his office after class because I was feeling lonely and insecure about my academic abilities. I have always been the kind of girl to put my friends, cheer team, and social life before my grades. That's not to say I'm dumb or whatever. I've always made at least a C in every class. But I can't pretend like I'm some academic genius or anything. That stuff has just never mattered much to me. But Mapletown College has a strict reputation for high grades, churning out brilliant minds every year. So for me, as an average student who came to this prestigious, pricey private school on a cheerleading scholarship, it can be really intimidating. I don't know anyone here, and even my own teammates have their own little clique, without me.

Professor Byron has been so helpful and comforting to me this semester, coaching me through some of the more difficult class material and convincing me that I am, in fact, smart enough to be here. He's gentle and patient with me like no teacher has been before, treating me almost more like a friend than a student. At first, we only met up once a week after class to talk about course material and stuff. Then it was twice a week. Then almost every school day. We started talking about a range of topics: not just class stuff but life stuff. Movies, TV shows, traveling, food, politics. All kinds of things. He's so damn smart, and it's sexy as hell. And what's more, he makes *me* feel smart, too. He has been a true godsend to me, and I think it's high time that I offer him something special in return.

I walk up to his office, which is a small separate building. He's so well-liked and connected here that his office is fancy and private, especially compared to some of the rest. Which makes my plan even easier to carry out. I knock on his door, taking a deep breath.

"Come in," he calls out in that deep, sexy voice.

Here goes nothing. I open the door and walk in, flouncing just a little. He does a double take at the sight of me in my uniform, and I can tell he's into it. Of course, he does a good job of covering it up. He gives me a smile and says, "Wow. I've never seen your uniform. I mean, I knew you were on the squad, but it was hard to imagine."

"So, you've tried imagining it, then?" I ask coyly, taking a seat across from him with his desk between us. A flicker of embarrassment crosses his face, but he laughs gently.

"No, no. Of course not. I just meant that whenever you're here, you're so smart and articulate, it's hard to remember that you're also a cheerleader," he says quickly.

"Cheerleaders can't also be smart?" I ask, tilting my head to one side. I bat my eyelashes and bite my lip, toying with him. He rakes his fingers back through that sexy graying hair, scoffing and smiling. Buying time. Stalling. I know I'm making him uncomfortable, and I love it.

"That's not what I meant," says the professor. "You know I value you as a student."

"I know. But um, how much?" I inquire innocently. He blinks in confusion.

"How much?" he repeats, frowning.

I stand up and walk over to stand in front of him, looking down into that handsome face while I twirl one of my long pigtails around my finger. "How much do you value me? Oh, as a student, of course," I add with a giggle.

He looks utterly stunned, frozen and afraid to move. "Well, if you really want to know, you've become a favorite student of mine, I'll admit. Don't tell your classmates, obviously."

I grin, pleased with his answer. "I won't tell if you don't tell," I whisper, leaning forward and putting my knee on his thigh. He looks totally flabbergasted.

"Miss Peters," Professor says, shaking his head. "I don't know what's going on."

"You never call me Miss Peters. It's Annabel," I laugh. "But if you want me to keep calling you professor, I'm fine with that. In fact, I think it's kind of hot."

"Annabel, I-I think maybe you've misunderstood our relationship here," he says, unconvincingly. I raise an eyebrow at him, pouting.

"Really? So you can tell me truthfully that you've never thought about me while you jack off in the shower in the morning? You don't picture me naked when you're lying in bed at night? Come on, Professor Byron. We've always been so honest with each other," I urge him.

His jaw tightens and his hands curl into fists. I can tell it's taking all his restraint not to reach out and touch me. I keep talking, determined to make him crack. "Professor, weren't you the one who told me that the reason you teach erotic lit at the start of a new semester is to grab your students' attention and make them stay interested?"

"Yes. I said that," he sighs.

"And did you not tell me that you liked to make your students open up and come out of their shells?" I egg him on.

"Yes, Annabel," he admits, staring openly at my tits.

"Well, this is me coming out of my shell. You said yourself that here at college, we're all equals. You're my professor, but you're not my dad. You're my... friend. I'm eighteen. I can make my own choices. You and I have talked a lot about some seriously racy subjects. But what good is it talking about Sappho and the innuendos in Shakespeare's poetry if it stops there? You're always encouraging us to think outside the box and think hard about our future. About what we really, truly want," I tell him firmly. "And what I really, truly want is for you to fuck me, Professor."

"Jesus," he swears, shaking his head. But there's a flicker of undeniable desire in his gorgeous eyes, and I know I've nabbed him. "Okay. I'll do this. But I'm wearing a condom."

"Of course. I'm not dumb enough to go bareback my first time, silly!" I laugh. I lean in and kiss him, softly at first, then harder. He moans, his hands holding me tight in place like he's afraid I might disappear into thin air at any moment.

"And that's not all," I add when I break away for a moment. "I want an audience. I want you to fuck me while another man watches."

"And who is this mystery voyeur you refer to, Annabel?" he asks, but there's a lilt of playfulness in his voice. I pick up his desk phone and hand it to him.

"Coach Robinson," I answer flatly. "He's always

watching me during practice. I know he wants me. He'll say yes. Just call him and ask before he heads home for the day. I don't want to wait anymore, Professor. I want you to take my virginity. Right here, right now."

Professor Byron stares at me for a long moment, sizing me up, as though he half-expects this to be an elaborate prank. But when he sees how serious I am, he wordlessly dials a number into his phone. When someone answers on the other end of the line, he says, "Coach? Is there a chance you could stop by my office? It's urgent."

He hangs up the phone and I lean forward, straddling his lap and wrapping my arms around his neck. He still looks positively shocked by the whole thing, but I know it's too late for him to back out. Besides, judging by the long, hard stiffness underneath me, I have a feeling he has no desire to stop. Only minutes later, there's a knock at the door and I get up to answer it. Coach looks completely surprised to see me there, blinking as though he doesn't believe his eyes.

He looks over at Professor Byron, shrugging in confusion. "Well? What's going on?"

Professor glances at me, giving a nod. I take Coach's hand and pull him into the room, locking the door behind him. I lead him over to the fancy sofa where I sat the very first time I came to this office to talk about course material.

"What is this?" Coach asks.

"I've noticed you watching me," I tell him.

"Is this some kind of intervention or something? I-I never meant to make you uncomfortable," he protests quickly. I giggle and roll my eyes.

"No, no. Don't worry. I love it when you watch me. I bet you get so hard watching me dance around in my little uniform. It turns me on, Coach. In fact, I want you to keep watching me. Right now," I tell him as I walk back over to Professor, who stands up and kisses me. I glance over to see Coach's mouth hanging open.

"What the hell," he mumbles, eyes wide.

Professor gives him a shrug. "Just go with it. This is what she wants. It would be a shame to turn away a student in need, right?" he says pointedly. Coach nods, looking like he just can't believe his good luck. Everything is going according to plan.

I step away for a moment and begin to turn slowly, shaking my ass, rolling my hips while I feel myself up. I never break eye contact with Professor Byron as I dance, biting my lip and watching as his eyes glaze over with desire. I begin to strip out of my uniform, peeling off my top to let my bouncy, perky tits fall free. I kick off my shoes and slowly take off my panties, leaving just my knee-high socks and flouncy little skirt. I dance over to Professor, who is now sitting down in the chair closest to me, watching with rapt attention.

I bend over and grind my tight little ass against his crotch, feeling his hard cock against me, turning me on while I seduce him. I glance over to see that Coach is stroking himself through his jeans, watching us closely. That gives me a little thrill of pleasure.

Professor can't hold back anymore. He grabs me and bends me over his lap, making me giggle with delight. He lifts up my skirt and smacks my ass, hard enough to leave a handprint. Hard enough to bring tears of pleasure to my eyes. I moan and wiggle my ass, urging him to do it again. He gropes my taut ass and slides his fingers along my wet slit, groaning with need.

"Fuck, you're so hot," he rumbles, feeling me up. I love the sensation of his huge hands on my body. He lifts me up and puts me back on his lap, straddling him. He kisses my lips, his tongue pushing into my mouth while he plays with my breasts, squeezing them and rolling my nipples between his fingers until I'm sighing with bliss.

"How long have you wanted to touch me like this?" I whisper as he lowers his mouth to my nipple, flicking his tongue over the stiffened peak. I moan and shiver at his warm tongue.

"Since the first day I saw you in my classroom," he admits, his hands slipping down between us. He finds my clit immediately, working it with two expert fingers while he sucks my breast. I toss my head back, my eyes closing as he massages my sensitive clit. I rut against him, starting to lose myself in the pleasure. Finally, I gush cum all over his fingers, and he lets out a satisfied groan.

"Good girl. Very good," he growls, swallowing down my whimpers and moans. He grabs me and stands up, walking me backward to pin me against the wall of bookshelves. Professor hikes my leg up over his waist while he licks and sucks my nipples, his hand slipping down to slide two long fingers inside my slick cunny.

"Oh my god," I gasp as he begins to thrust his fingers in and out of me, hard and fast. I've never felt anything like this before. It's almost too much to handle.

I look over to see that Coach has unzipped his

jeans and is stroking his massive, hard shaft, watching us with an animalistic hunger on his handsome face. I lock eyes with him while Professor fingers my tight little hole, and even when I gush my honey again and again, I never break eye contact. Coach strokes himself faster, groaning with pleasure at the sight of the cum dripping down my thighs. Then Byron leads me over to the sofa, sitting down at the opposite end from Coach. He pulls me down, unzipping his pants to let his huge cock spring free.

"Suck my cock, Annabel," he commands. "Now. I want to feel those soft lips around me." Dripping wet, I climb onto the couch and bend down to suck his cock into my mouth, reveling in the way his size stretches my cheeks. Meanwhile, Coach has my slick pussy right in his face. I shake my ass a little bit, teasing him as I take Professor's cock down to the hilt.

"Fuck. Just like that, baby," he groans, pushing my head down slightly. I begin to bob up and down on his cock, sucking and flicking my tongue over the tight head of his shaft. I can almost feel the temptation building in Coach. I know he wants to touch me. And I've decided that I want him to touch me, too. Just watching isn't enough. I want both men at once.

Almost like he can read my mind, Coach leans in, grabbing my ass to hold me still while he licks my slick pussy. I moan and rut back against him, riding his face, his flicking tongue, while I deepthroat Professor's cock. Coach moans, lapping up my creamy cum as he buries his face in my cunny, circling my over-stimulated clit with his tongue until I'm weak with pleasure. He suckles my clit, devouring my pussy and making me nearly choke on Professor's dick, until finally I squirt my honey into his mouth. He groans, lapping up every drop.

"Turn around. Suck his cock," Professor orders me, pushing me off. I obey him without a moment's hesitation, turning around to lower myself down and pull Coach's cock into my mouth. He leans back and groans, resting his hand on the back of my head while I bob up and down. Professor walks over to his desk and takes out a little bottle of something, as well as two small square packets. He comes back over and sits down on the sofa, with my ass in his face. He squirts something cool and wet onto my tight asshole and begins to rub little circles around it while he fucks my pussy with his other hand. Slowly, he begins to slip his finger inside my ass, which only intensifies the sensation of his fingers in my cunt. It feels overwhelmingly stimulating. Almost too much to handle. I never imagined I would enjoy anything or anyone near my ass, but I'm surprised at how good it feels. I moan, sending thrums of vibrations up through Coach's body.

Professor fingers my asshole and my cunny at the same time, making me shiver and gasp with pleasure. I rut back against him while I pump Coach's cock with my hand and lips, stroking him harder and faster. I want him to lose control. I want them both to feel as good as I feel right now. Coach reaches around to play with my tits, squeezing them and brushing his fingers over my nipples. I moan and rock back against Professor's fingers, pushing them deeper inside me until he brushes against my g-spot and I cum again, nearly collapsing with bliss.

"You like that, hmm?" he says, and I can hear how pleased he is to have made me cum so many times.

I moan, "Mhm," as I nearly gag myself on Coach's dick.

"You want more, Annabel?" Professor asks.

"Mhm!" I respond enthusiastically, my mouth still full of cock.

"I'm going to fuck this tight little virgin cunt until you're squirming," he growls. I tremble with anticipation, wiggling my ass and tantalizing him. Professor gets up on his knees, slides a condom on over his cock, and presses the head against my quivering cunt.

The anticipation is nearly killing me. I look back at him, pleading. "Fuck me, Professor Byron. Take me. I want you to take my virginity. Please."

"That's exactly what I wanted to hear," he grunts, grabbing hold of my hips and shoving his massive cock deep inside my cunt. I cry out, losing myself to pleasure as he thrusts into me again and again, hard and fast. He strikes against my g-spot every time, and I'm almost too overcome with stimulation to suck Coach's cock. Coach notices this, and soon he decides it's his turn. Both men switch, with Coach rolling a condom on over his cock and fucking me in the pussy while I suck Professor's dick, moaning and trembling with need. Coach grabs my pigtails while he fucks me from behind, slamming into me and groaning.

"Fuck, your pussy is so tight," he snarls. He picks me up and turns me around, leaning back so that I'm on top, riding his cock. Professor stands up and watches us for a few minutes, stroking his cock, biding his time. Coach reaches around and fingers my asshole while he fucks me, sending me over the edge. I cum again, soaking his cock with my honey.

"You like a finger in your ass, little girl?" Professor growls.

"Yes, sir," I murmur breathlessly.

"Would you like something bigger than that? Would you like a cock in your pussy and your ass at the same time?" he asks.

I nod vigorously, unable to believe what he's suggesting.

Coach lifts me up, holding me up easily while he pounds into my slick cunny. Professor comes up behind me, slowly working his thick cock into my tight asshole. The two men hold me up like I weigh nothing at all, both cocks sliding in and out of me until I'm gasping and wailing with pleasure.

"Oh--my--god!" I squeal, cumming over and over again from the combined pleasure of two hard, massive cocks inside me. This is far better than anything I've ever dreamed of. Far better than my wildest fantasies. Two of the hottest older men in the world, sharing me, fucking me mercilessly right here in the office. My cum drips down between us, staining the carpet in a little puddle while I shudder through one climax after another.

"You love these big cocks in your tight little holes, don't you?" Coach snarls in my ear.

"Yes, Coach! I fucking love it," I gasp.

"You want us to fill your little pussy and asshole with cum?" Professor asks, quickening his pace. I nod and dive forward to capture his lips in a desperate kiss. I know they're wearing condoms, but it doesn't matter. I want them to pump me full of their cum. I want them to explode in my tight virgin holes.

"Please! Fuck me harder," I beg them. "I want you to lose control. I've been such a good girl all semester. Please. I've worked hard for this. I want your cum inside me."

That's all it takes.

Coach and Professor both cum inside me at the same time, both men bellowing my name as they clutch me close between them, all of us dripping with my honey, all of us shuddering with over-whelming pleasure. After a few minutes of breathing raggedly and clinging to each other, they put me down, each one kissing me deeply. We get dressed, all glowing and excited.

Before I leave for the night, we all agree to make this a regular occurrence. Sex that mindblowing can't possibly just happen once.

"*G*o team!" I exclaim, jumping up and down, waving my pom-poms with a huge grin on my face. The crowds in the stands are going wild, because the Tornadoes just scored the winning touchdown. The night air is brisk and lovely, the moon shining down as the team rushes off field to celebrate. And now that my routine is over, I turn and rush into the waiting arms of Professor Byron, who has been sitting in the bleachers behind the squad the whole time. He picks me up and swings me around, kissing me passionately.

"That was amazing, baby," he says, caressing my cheek lovingly. That softness in his eyes just melts me every time. "I'm sorry it'll be your last routine for awhile, but you know what the doctor said."

I roll my eyes and laugh. "I know, I know. Don't worry, after tonight, I'll be retiring my cheerleading uniform for a while. At least until after the baby is born," I tell him.

"It's all about what's good for you. And the baby," he adds.

"Besides, I don't think I'd look very cute in my uniform with my big pregnant belly poking out," I giggle. He kisses me again, sweetly.

"You would look even more beautiful than you do now," Professor says, wrapping me up in a tight hug. Coach comes running over, looking exhilarated. This is a big win for the team. A great win for his career. Professor greets him with a warm hello, and I turn to hug him, kissing him on the cheek.

"You did it, babe!" I exclaim happily.

"Oh no, the team did it. I'm just here to guide them. And cheer them on. But not as well as you do," Coach adds with a wink. "You looked beautiful out there, Annabel."

"Thanks, Coach," I answer, biting my lip.

Both men put an arm around me as we walk away from the field. The squad will have their own little celebration, as well as the football team. Hell, the whole college is celebrating a win like this one. But as for me? I know I have something much more exciting waiting for me at home, with my two guys who love me.

PUNISHING HER

I'm lying in my roommates' bathtub, the big, lavish soaking tub I've filled to the brim with a lavender-scented bubble bath. My toes poke out of the water at the porcelain edge, and I can feel the hot water warming my body and helping me relax.

There are scented candles flickering on the counter for an added dose of atmosphere, and a glass of wine in my hand. I can't help but feel a little turned on, totally naked and making cheeky faces at the camera set up on the counter, carefully pointed downward to capture my every pose and kiss I blow in its direction.

I know these are going to be a particularly saucy set of photos for me to post on my account, and I am certain that many of my male fans will get off to it. I may seem ditzy, since that's all part of the act, but I'm not stupid. I know exactly what my fans want from me. More sex appeal, all the time.

Some girls might shrink away from all that pressure, but not me. I lean into it.

It arouses me to think that when I post these photos later, a bunch of random strangers will stop whatever they're doing and go hide in their bathroom stalls at work and jerk off to the thought of me. I am their fantasy, and I live to tantalize my followers. My free hand is hidden underneath the thick layer of floral-scented bubbles, sliding over my wet, soapy nipples. They're perky and sensitive, making me sigh when I play with them.

I bite my lip and wink at the camera, turning my head from side to side and making sure my hair doesn't slip out of its elaborate, perfectly-designed messy bun. It's all about looking effortless, even though there is actually a lot of effort happening here. It's hard work making life look so easy. I'm basically a walking, talking, smiling billboard in the form of a hot young blonde.

My real name is Kenzie Walton, but I am much more popularly known as KenzieKitten1999. That is what over one million devoted followers call me on my Instagram account. I am basically one gigantic promotional ad. I advertise a lifestyle, a fantasy my followers can only dream about.

My account is chock full of sexy, smiley images meant to show off how amazing and fulfilling my life is. I post photos of beautifully-arrange flowers, rainbow-hued acai smoothie bowls complete with frozen berries and gourmet chocolate. I always have either a fancy pink cocktail or an expensive coconut water in my hand.

It doesn't matter that I'm nineteen, so it's not even legal for me to drink a cocktail yet. I have a fake ID, plus if I make the drink look delicious and photogenic enough, I can always lie and say it's alcoholic even if it's not.

It's all about the illusion, anyway. People believe what they want to believe. And my followers? They want to believe I am the sun-soaked, joyful, blonde angel of their wildest dreams. So that is the image I sell them. I'm always wearing a flouncy sun dress that hints at my flawless, curvy body, or a bikini, which leaves almost nothing to the imagination. I work hard to keep in shape. I haven't touched a carb in months. I work out at the gym super early in the morning, when no one else is there.

And yeah, I do go out to clubs on a nearly nightly

basis, but it's mostly because dancing is a great way to burn calories.

Besides, I need to snap cute selfies of myself on the dance floor or on the rooftop VIP lounge, looking gorgeous and tipsy, smiling with a group of friends who I have hand-selected for their good looks and trendy style. I need to associate with the best and brightest stars this city has to offer.

That's why I left my tiny, quiet hometown in Arkansas and moved out west to Los Angeles: I want to be a star. Of course, my ultimate goal is to be an actress, but for now, I'm a part-time model and full-time Instagram influencer, which I think is kind of like an acting role in itself. I have to show my audience what they want to see, and hide the parts that would detract from my carefully-curated image.

Which is why I have to pretend like this is my bathroom and my bathtub, even though it's actually the one my two roommates, Seth and Hayden, share.

I have my own bathroom, of course, but it's not as fancy as this one. They get the big tub, plus the lighting in here is so much better. I'm sure they would be pissed off to see me in here, but I don't care. I do whatever I want. I'm used to getting my way. I was always a daddy's girl growing up, and my dad spoiled me like crazy. It was difficult to leave him and all my friends behind in Arkansas, but I'm determined to make it here in California.

Part of the image I'm trying to cultivate for my adoring fans is that I live a life of wealth and leisure. Having to live with two roommates kind of destroys that fantasy. So, I pretend like the whole beautiful beach-side condo belongs to me. And to be honest? It kind of does. I'm the boss. I know I can be a little bratty sometimes, but it's only because I'm the princess of this castle, and everyone should know it.

Besides, I can't pretend like it doesn't turn me on a little bit, lying here in the bathtub where my two hot roommates get naked.

Hayden is twenty-four years old, a professional surfer, and super athletic and muscular. He wins all kinds of competitions and stuff, and he's always working out and going for long jogs to stay in shape. Seth is twenty-eight, and supposedly he's some kind of amateur filmmaker or whatever like every other guy out here in LA, but he works as a graphic design artist to pay the bills.

Both of them are smoking hot.

Tall, dark hair, gorgeous eyes-- Hayden has a perpetual surfer tan and Seth wears those adorable dorky black-rimmed glasses. I would never admit it to them, but I would fuck either one of them in a heartbeat. I turn off the camera, satisfied with the photos I've taken, and sink back down under the hot bubbly water with a sigh.

I close my eyes and let my hands roam down my body, caressing my supple breasts, my taut stomach, down to my pussy. I bite my lip as I touch myself, imagining Seth and Hayden walking in and finding me here in their bathroom, violating their boundaries. Maybe they would be so angry that they'd want to punish me. Teach me a lesson.

I begin to massage my clit in little circles, moaning as I picture Hayden unzipping his jeans and whipping out his cock, stroking it while he stares at me with those dark eyes. I imagine him getting into the bathtub with me, the two of us soapy and slippery as we make out. Seth would come up behind me, pressing his cock against my ass while he kisses my neck. I roll my hips in rhythm, sighing as I get closer and closer to climax. I play with my nipples while I touch myself, picturing Hayden's face as he slides his cock inside my virgin pussy…

"Fuck," I murmur breathlessly as I cum all over my fingers underneath the water. I lie there for a moment, just coming down from the waves of pleasure. It feels amazing, but it doesn't totally satisfy me. I need more, and it's killing me. But I'm way too busy to date anyone. I haven't even kissed a guy since I was in high school a couple years ago. It's so weird how I make everyone think I'm this sexy siren, but in real life, I'm alone.

I get out of the bath and dry off, then check the time on my phone. "Oh my god!" I gasp, realizing I'm late for an audition I booked last week. I can't miss this.

I hurriedly get dressed and head out, hopping into my little pink Honda. I rush across town to the casting set, my stomach twisting in nervous knots. I hope this goes well, because this film could be the one to catapult me into true stardom. I'm in a waiting room with a bunch of other pretty girls, all of whom give me dirty looks and ignore me. It's a cutthroat world, and I'm used to it by now. Finally, the casting director calls me into the room and hands me a script to read off of while I give the camera sultry looks. I do a pretty damn good job, if I do say so myself, and at the end, the director agrees.

"That was amazing, Miss Walton," he says, walking over to shake my hand. He gives me the same lusty onceover that all men give me, and I know he's picturing me naked. It's difficult not to. I give him a demure smile.

"Thank you so much for the opportunity," I reply.

"Sure thing," he says. He's still staring at me like I'm a piece of meat. I'm used to it. "I hope I'll be seeing more of you soon."

I giggle flirtatiously and toss my hair over my shoulder. "I hope so, too."

With that, I head back out of the building, passing by all the other wannabe actresses in the lobby. I'm feeling good. That went really well. I check my phone to see a ton of new notifications, most of which I expected. But I also have a message from my roommate, Seth. It says: *Can you come home soon? We need to have a roommate meeting. It's important.*

I frown at the phone, confused as to what he means. They were out all day today, but I guess they came home while I was in the audition room. Regardless, I do not like being told what to do. Sure, we'll have that meeting, but I'm going to take my time getting home! So I ignore his text and drive to my favorite nail salon to get a manicure, then hit up a trendy coffee shop to grab a skinny latte before finally heading back home with the sun slipping down over the horizon. By the time I pull into the parking space in front of the condo, it's almost sunset.

I come waltzing into the condo with my freshly-painted nails and fancy latte to find Seth and Hayden standing in the living room, giving me very stern looks. I respond with an innocent smile and take a sip of my drink.

"What took you so long? We've been waiting for you," Seth says angrily.

"What's the big deal? You said we needed to have a meeting, but you didn't say when," I reply brattily. Hayden glares at me, his muscular arms folded over his broad chest.

"Are you kidding me? We said it was important," he retorts. "In fact, you know what? This is exactly the problem. You're so selfish and stubborn you just do whatever you want without thinking of others at all."

"I don't know what you're talking about," I respond with a shrug.

"Yes, you do. You make messes all the time and never clean up after yourself. You eat our food without replacing it or paying for it. You use our soap and towels and stuff without asking. You have your own room and bathroom, and yet you insist on using our stuff! You walk around the apartment dressed like a slut, just to tease us." Seth accuses fiercely.

"You go out all hours of the night, waking me up

when you come home. I'm an athlete, Kenzie. I need my sleep," Hayden insists.

"Oh, whatever. You guys are just ganging up on me," I protest, pouting.

"So, you're denying it? All of it?" Hayden asks, raising an eyebrow.

I nod. "Yep. I don't have any idea what you're talking about."

Seth and Hayden exchange smug looks. Seth grabs the TV remote and turns on the television, then presses play. On the screen is a familiar sight... me! Walking into the kitchen and stealing their granola bars. Lying on Seth's bed and taking selfies in my bra and panties. And then footage from this morning, when I touched myself while taking a bath in their bathroom!

"Oh my god, I can't believe you guys filmed me! This is illegal, you know? This is blackmail!" I shout angrily.

Seth smirks. "You're damn right it is, and if we leaked the footage, it could ruin your career, couldn't it?"

"Yes, it could," I shoot back.

"It would be a real shame if your followers got to see the real Kenzie Walton. Parading around the house in her panties, being an entitled little brat," Hayden insinuates.

My heart is pounding. "Okay, okay. Fine. You got me. But please, please don't post that footage. I'll do anything. Whatever you want. I'll stop messing with your stuff, I swear," I tell them desperately. They grin at each other.

"You've teased us for too long," Hayden says in a low voice. "I know you did it on purpose. You just love seeing us lust after you, don't you?"

I stare down at the floor, ashamed at how easily they can read me. "Yes," I murmur.

"Well, tonight you're going to be punished for that. You've pushed us too far," Seth says.

"What do you mean?" I ask, confused.

Hayden points to his bedroom. "Get in there. You like messing around in my room so much, go ahead." I reluctantly walk into the bedroom, with Seth and Hayden following me. Seth locks the door and Hayden walks up to me with a mischievous smile.

"Take off your clothes," he commands. I blush.

"What?" I gasp. "Are you kidding me?"

"I'm serious," Hayden says. "Strip for us."

With my heart racing wildly, I obey his command. I unzip my dress and let it fall to the floor, standing in front of them in just my pink bra and panties.

"Keep going. No need to be shy now, Kenz. We've already seen you masturbating in the bathtub. I always knew you were a dirty girl," Seth growls. "Take off the rest, and do it slowly. You like to tease us so much, so give us a strip tease."

As frightened as I am, I can't help but be a little turned on. I have had so many fantasies about my roommates. Fucking me. Punishing me. This isn't what I expected, but I'm beginning to look forward to whatever they have in store for me. I sway my hips, slowly undulating as I unclasp my bra and toss it aside, then seductively pull off my panties and drop them, too.

"Damn, you're fucking hot," Hayden swears, shaking his head in awe. "You want to be a star, right? Well, we've got a role for you to play."

Seth pulls out his cell phone and holds it up to record me standing naked in front of them. I gasp, instinctively trying to cover myself up. But then Hayden walks over to me and picks me up in his arms, tossing me onto his bed. I'm lying on my stomach, with Seth filming as Hayden pulls me over his lap and begins spanking me, hard.

I cry out in pain and Hayden smiles devilishly.

"This is your punishment. You want to act like a brat? You'll be dealt with like a brat," he snarls. He smacks my ass again, making me squirm with pain, even though I can feel my pussy getting wet.

"You like that, dirty girl?" Seth sneers, leaning in closer with the camera. I look up at him with pleading eyes, whimpering as Hayden spanks me again and again. I know he's got to be leaving red welts on my skin, and for some reason the thought of that just turns me on even more. Finally, Hayden pushes me off his lap and drags me up to the head-board of his bed. He lifts up my wrists, tying them to the bed posts on either side of me so that I'm restrained. I watch him curiously, trying to figure out what he's going to do to me next.

Hayden kisses me as his hands rove down my body, squeezing lightly at my throat before traveling down further to fondle my full breasts, rolling my nipples between his fingers and making me moan with pleasure. "Oh, you like that?" he hisses. I nod vigorously. He grins and leans in to suck and nip at my breasts, flicking his tongue over my nipples until I'm crying out with need. Then, Seth climbs onto the bed, too, lowering himself down between my thighs. He begins to slide his wet, warm tongue up and down my wet folds,

CANDY QUINN

sucking on my clit while Hayden plays with my tits.

"Oh my god," I whimper. "It feels so good."

Seth licks my pussy faster, circling my sensitive clit with his tongue until I'm bucking against his face, straining in my wrist ties, desperate for a release. But every time I get close, he backs off, taking me all the way to the brink and then stopping just before I can cum. Hayden kisses and sucks my neck, leaving bright purple bruises on my skin while he gropes my breasts.

"Please, please. I need to cum," I moan. "You're driving me crazy."

"Good," Hayden growls. "Now you know what we feel like."

"You can have anything you want. Just let me cum," I beg him.

"That's exactly what I wanted to hear," Hayden replies. Seth stops eating me out and walks into the shared en suite bathroom. He comes back out holding my vibrator! I forgot that I left it in there earlier. But before I even get a chance to feel embarrassed, Hayden takes the vibrator and turns it up to the highest, most intense setting, and presses it directly against my clit. Seth comes at me from the other side, shoving two long fingers inside my tight, virginal cunt. I let out a scream of pain and pleasure as Seth fingerfucks my pussy and Hayden rubs the vibrator in tight, burning circles around my clit. It feels so good I can hardly stand it, paralyzed and unable to stop them even as the sensations become so overwhelming it almost stings.

"Oh my god, oh my god," I whisper breathlessly, my whole body starting to shake. Seth fingers me harder and faster, striking at a deep, delicious spot inside me while the pleasure builds higher and higher.

"Cum for me, Kenzie. Cum all over his fingers," Hayden commands.

With a shriek of intense pleasure, I feel my pussy gush sweet, sticky honey all over Seth's hand. "Oh fuck, yes," he snarls, lifting his soaked fingers to his mouth and sucking up every drop of my cum.

"Not done with you yet," Hayden says. "We're just getting started."

Both guys get up and strip out of their clothes, showing off their muscular bodies and long, hard cocks. I gasp at the sight of them-- both of them are massive! I feel my pussy aching at the sight of them. Hayden stands up on the bed and walks over to straddle my face, shoving his thick cock in my mouth before I can even fully process what is happening. He holds me still, slowly sliding the full length of his shaft down my throat while I sit perfectly still, in shock. I've never had a cock in any of my holes before. I've never even touched a man's cock until now.

"Yeah, that's right, Kenzie. Suck my fucking cock," Hayden hisses, gradually thrusting a little faster and deeper into my mouth. His rod is so huge that it brushes the back of my throat, making me cough. "Choke on it, you dirty little slut," he commands.

I never knew the sensation of a cock in my mouth could feel so good. Tasting his salty precum, flicking my tongue along the velvety underside of his shaft, letting his immense size gag me-- it's so hot I can hardly stand it. And just when I think it can't get more intense, Seth begins to massage something cool and slippery around my tight little asshole. I flinch at first, but then he presses the vibrator against my clit while he slides a finger inside my ass. All the while, Hayden is fucking my throat, thrusting hard into my mouth until my cheeks are aching. The vibrator on my clit feels so overwhelming along with the new, strangely delicious feeling of something sliding in and out of my ass and my throat stuffed with thick cock. He slips in

SHARING HER

another finger, then two, until he's rapidly fucking my ass with his fingers as the vibrator sends shock-waves of intense pleasure through my body. I moan and whimper, unable to speak with Hayden's shaft down my throat, and I cum over and over again, gushing all over the bedsheets.

"Good girl," Seth whispers. "Cum for me, baby. Give me all that sweet honey."

He drops the vibrator and holds up the cell phone again, giving my pussy a close up as cum leaks out. "What a pretty little pink pussy. So gorgeous," he says.

"I think it's time I shove my cock inside that little cunt, don't you?" Hayden growls. I look up at him pleadingly, begging him to fuck my aching cunny. He takes his cock out of my mouth, unties my bruised wrists, and orders, "Get on your knees."

I hurriedly obey, shaking my ass a little bit and biting my lip. They've turned me into a filthy little sex kitten, and I don't even care. All I care about right now is getting those thick, glorious cocks deep inside me. Seth moves up to position himself in front of me, and I hungrily suck his cock into my mouth, moaning at the taste of the little bead of cum on the tip. Holding the camera in place to film me sucking his cock, he groans and strokes my hair, sliding his long, hard shaft in and out of my mouth while Hayden slips back behind me, rubbing the head of his cock in circles around my slick little pussy. He's teasing me, just like I have been teasing them for the whole year we've lived here together. I deserve it.

And I want it more than anything.

"I bet this little virgin pussy is just starving for a thick cock, isn't it?" Hayden snarls.

I moan and press back against him, urging him to hurry up and fuck me. He chuckles darkly and grabs hold of my hips, thrusting into my tight cunny in one swift, hard movement. I cry out in pain, seeing stars as Hayden immediately starts fucking me faster and faster. He's not being gentle at all, throwing caution to the wind as he slams into my little aching cunt, popping my cherry and making me whimper with mingled agony and pleasure.

Seth picks up the pace, too, fucking my throat nearly as hard as Hayden fucks my pussy. Hayden smacks my ass hard, groaning with beast-like need. It's like he's a wild animal, losing control and not giving a single fuck about whether it hurts me or not. But instead of being afraid, I'm just so turned on. I want these boys to use me and abuse me, treat me like the little sexpot all my followers think I am. I want to feel them explode inside me, pump me full of their cum. I don't care if it's in my pussy, my mouth, or my asshole. I just want them to fill me up and make me their own. Hayden fucks me harder, the tip of his cock spearing into my g-spot over and over, making me tremble and moan, sending vibrations up through Seth's shaft in my mouth.

"God, you're so fucking tight," Hayden hisses through gritted teeth. "Such an innocent little virgin. I bet you've never even dreamed of being fucked like this. A cock in your mouth, a cock in your sweet little cunt."

Seth pulls my hair, yanking my head back a little as he shoves his cock further down my throat, making me gag. It's so fucking hot that I cry out, my cum squirting all over Hayden's shaft, covering him in my warm honey.

"Oh, good girl. Good girl," Seth groans. "You love being choked with cock, don't you?"

I can only whimper and tremble in response, my whole body going weak. Hayden thrusts into me a few more times before pulling out and slapping my ass. Seth does the same, taking his cock out of my mouth. Both men get off the bed and I turn over on my back, confused as to why they've stopped. Hayden smirks.

"Don't worry, my sweet little slut, we're not done with you yet," he assures me. Seth holds up the camera and Hayden walks over to stand by the bed. "Touch yourself like you did in the bathtub. I want to see you rub your clit for me."

I reach down and obediently begin to massage my clit, moaning and bucking my hips. Seth leans in closer with the camera, recording a close up of my fingers circling my over-sensitized little bundle of pleasure, working myself closer and closer to yet another climax. But Hayden won't let me get off so easily.

"Don't cum. You're not allowed to cum yet," he commands.

"But it feels so good," I pout, gasping for breath. "I need to cum. Please."

"No. Not yet. This is your punishment. You will only cum when I say so," he orders firmly. I lie back against the pillows, watching my two sexy room-mates stroke their cocks and watch me touch myself on camera. It's so overwhelmingly dirty, being watched like this. I'm so close to cumming, but Hayden pushes my hand away and pins both arms over my head before I can climax. I let out a little whine and he grins.

"Oh, I've got something even better in store for

you, Kenzie," he warns. He shoves his cock inside my cunt again, making me moan and squirm. Seth, still holding the camera in one hand, picks up the vibrator and presses it hard against my clit again while Hayden fucks me harder and faster.

"Oh fuck, oh fuck," I gasp, my eyes rolling back in my head. I can't stand it anymore.

"Cum for me, Kenzie. Cum all over this hard cock," Hayden demands, and I explode with a gush of honey, shivering and weak. I'm so overwhelmed I can hardly stand it. Hayden pulls out and Seth steps in, fucking my tight little cunt while Hayden massages my clit with the vibrator. It burns like hell, but the pain only makes the pleasure even sweeter. They switch again, only this time Hayden slowly and carefully pushes his enormous shaft inside my asshole.

"Oh god, it hurts," I hiss, tears burning in my eyes.

"But it feels good, too, doesn't it?" Hayden growls.

I nod. "Yes. Oh, yes. Oh my god," I scream as he fucks my ass harder and harder. He rubs the vibrator up and down my slick cunny while his cock slides in and out of my asshole, striking deep within me. Even though he's fucking my ass, I can feel every thrust in my aching pussy. Seth films us closely as he gropes and fondles my breasts, adding just another shock of pleasure to the mix. Hayden thrusts into my ass harder and harder, until it feels like he might break me in half, his hands grasping my hips to hold me in place while he uses my body.

"I bet you've never even dreamed of having a cock in your tight little ass, huh?" Hayden snarls, that fire burning in his dark eyes again. "Tell me, do you like it, Kenzie?"

"Yes!" I cry out, clutching at the bedsheets on either side of me.

"Such a dirty little slut, letting me fuck your asshole. God, you're so tight. You're going to make me cum, Kenzie. Is that what you want? You want me to fill up your tight little hole with my cum?" he teases me. I nod, biting my lip.

"Please. Oh god, please cum in my ass, Hayden," I gasp.

"What do you think, Seth? Do you think she deserves cum in her little asshole?" he says.

Seth grins. "Yeah, I think she's earned it."

"I agree. I think she needs it, too. Don't you, Kenzie?" Hayden leers.

"Yes, yes, yes," I murmur breathlessly. "I need it."

Hayden picks up the pace, ramming his cock

deep inside my ass until I'm twitching with pain and pleasure, and just as I'm about to cum again, he rears back and slams into me one more time. "Fuck!" he shouts as his thick, hot cum explodes inside of me. He gives me a few swift, final thrust and then withdraws, letting his seed slowly leak out of my asshole while I lie there panting and overwhelmed. Seth hands the phone camera to Hayden and they switch places so that Seth can push his thick cock inside my twitching cunny.

"Oh my god," I whine, licking my lips he fucks my pussy.

"That's right, Kenzie," Seth growls. "You're going to have your ass and your cunt filled with cum. You like that? You want me to fill your sweet little hole with my cum?"

"Yes! Give it to me," I exclaim, clenching my pussy to bring him closer and closer to climax. I roll my hips, meeting his every thrust while he begins to lose control.

"Oh fuck. Just like that, baby," Seth hisses. "You know who you belong to?"

"You," I whisper. "You and Hayden."

"Exactly," Hayden says, leaning down to kiss me just as my cunt convulses with another intense orgasm. I moan into his mouth while Seth grunts appreciatively, feeling the way my twitching cunt squeezes his cock. He fucks me faster and more erratically, the rhythm getting out of control as he gets closer to cumming.

Then, he rams his cock inside me and holds it there, groaning with pleasure when his cock squirts hot, sticky seed deep within my cunt. He pulls out and rubs the slick head of his cock all over my clit, making me squirm and whimper. Both men shower me with kisses and caresses before Hayden carries me into the bathroom and sets me down in the bath. In the afterglow of the best sex I've ever even dreamed of, both of my handsome boys bathe me gently, caring for me while we all come down from the high.

~

"*A*nd cut!" yells Seth.

I sigh and give the crowd of cameramen, fellow actors, and other crew members a smile while they applaud a scene well done. Once the cameras stop rolling, Seth comes walking over to me and pulls me into a tight hug, kissing me on the forehead.

"That was amazing," he tells me genuinely. "I

think that's just exactly how that scene was meant to be played. And your eyes! God, that dress really makes the blue stand out on camera. I think this one is going to be Oscar bait, I'm telling you."

"Well, I think that has more to do with your awesome directing than my acting," I tell him, leaning my head on his shoulder as we walk off the set for a break. "Have you heard from Hayden yet about lunch? I'm starving," I add, just as my stomach growls loudly.

Seth laughs and hugs me. "He'll be here soon. He went to that burger place you like."

"Yes! That's exactly what I'm craving. God, how do you guys just read my mind like that?" I giggle, shaking my head in awe at my two sexy guys. Both of them spoil me to death, treating me like the princess I am. It's been three months since that fateful night when Hayden and Seth decided to "punish" me for how much of a brat I was being to them, and life could not be any sweeter. I ended up landing the role I auditioned for, and even though at first I had a problem with the casting director getting a little handsy with me, all of that was solved when Seth got hired on as assistant director. So both of us have fallen right into our dream jobs, and the best part is that we get to work together. As for

Hayden, he just secured a contract as a spokesman for a nationwide gym, shooting commercials and getting his photos taken for magazines left and right. He still surfs all the time, and he's actually been teaching me how to surf, too.

Just then, Hayden comes walking into the building carrying a gigantic take-out bag. I rush over to him excitedly and plant a big kiss on his cheek. "Hi, baby! How did the shoot go?" I ask him, rifling through the bag of food to find my burger.

"It was great. Especially with those tips you gave me on my poses," Hayden says, grinning. "What about you? Seth said the filming is going well."

"It is," I answer just as I take a big bite of my cheeseburger. "Everything is actually ahead of schedule, believe it or not."

"And that's a good thing, since you're going to start showing any minute now," Seth points out, laying a hand on my stomach. "We're in a race against time: film as much as possible before the baby makes her presence known."

Hayden laughs. "Well, hopefully things keep moving along, then."

"I hope so," I reply. And so far, things are awesome. I finally get to be an actress, Seth gets to be a filmmaker, Hayden's career is taking off, the baby is healthy and growing well, and my Instagram following skyrocketed the second I was picked for this role. I no longer have to lie and pretend I live by myself: now my followers get to see how truly happy I am, living with the two sexiest men in the world, who spoil me and take care of me. I never really did learn my lesson, though. I still use their stuff and prance around the house in my lingerie whenever I want to. The only difference now is that Seth and Hayden don't mind. I'm their girlfriend, and we share everything. In fact, I can't wait to share the rest of my life with them, happy and surrounded by love.

BLINDFOLDING HER

$\mathcal{T}$his is happening. This is working.

I'm lying on my bed, watching the bids roll in, the dollar amounts stretching higher before my eyes. I am so glad that my housemate isn't home right now, because I definitely don't want anyone to catch me doing this. Especially considering what I'm wearing.

I've always been a good girl, the type to wear sports bras and panties that cover me up, no-nonsense cotton in flat, plain colors. But right now? I'm wearing lingerie. With lace and cute little bows and everything. I can only imagine how enraged and offended my parents would be if they found out.

I gently squeeze my breasts through the fabric of my brand new, baby-pink push-up bra. There's a tiny white bow in between my full breasts, and I think maybe that's there to indicate that my tits are a gift. Or a prize of some kind. I have never thought much about my breasts, to be perfectly honest. The way I was raised, I never thought my physical appearance had much value. I take care of myself, of course, but I've always been so modest and demure.

Heck, even when I strip down to take a shower, I try not to look at my own reflection, just in case I get dirty thoughts about my own naked body! I have never touched myself *down there* before. I don't even know what it would feel like. I've been tempted from time to time in the past, when I watched a movie with an especially cute leading man or something. But I always stopped myself before I could do something really, truly sinful.

Which is why it's so dirty what I'm doing right now. One of my hands trails down my body, over my full, soft breasts, my taut stomach and curvaceous hips, down to the little mound between my legs. I hold my breath nervously as I cup my pussy. I have never put anything here, not even my own hand, until now. Even in the privacy of my own bedroom here, in my college town away from home, I feel like someone might walk in on me and tattle-tale to my parents about what a dirty little slut I am.

But who cares what they think anyway? It feels good, rubbing my sensitive clit through the lacy fabric of my panties. They match my bra almost perfectly, the same shade of ballerina-pink with tiny white bows. It feels like this lingerie was made for me. It's almost like my mysterious suitors can read my mind. I wonder if they know me in real life. Maybe we've already met somewhere before, and I just can't remember their faces or names...

I rub my clit slowly, breathing deeply as I fondle my breasts. Every time my fingers pass over my nipple, it sends a little spiral of pleasure down through my body. I can't believe I'm actually doing this: it's so sinful. I grew up afraid to even look at boys, for fear that small act would give me impure thoughts. My parents always taught me that the most valuable asset I can offer the world is my purity. My innocence. I have been lectured since day one about how I have to guard my virginity. I have only this one special gift to give, and once I give it away, I can never get it back. That's what Mom and Daddy taught me, anyway.

I close my eyes and imagine what my two guys must look like. There are have been many bidders, but those two stand out above the rest. I bet they're both a little bit older, more distinguished. Mature.

Responsible. I mean, they'd have to be, since they have so much disposable income to throw around, right? When I put my virginity up for auction in an ad on MyCampusList, my college's secret website for buying, selling, and meeting up with people, I never expected to get more than a couple hits. I did it out of desperation, thinking maybe I could eke out a few bucks to throw into the massive black hole of debt I'm about to incur.

You see, I've never had to worry much about money. My parents never let me have a job in high school. When they sent me here to Marysvale College, a private university, they were paying my tuition. That is, until they found out that I recently attended one little frat party that got out of hand. I wasn't even misbehaving, though. I'm underage, so I didn't have a single drop of alcohol. I chatted with some classmates, but I didn't do any dirty dancing or heavy petting. I was a good girl. Like always.

But they don't believe me. My parents are convinced I'm a party-crazed, filthy little slut now. So they cut me off. I took up a job as a barista, but I'm hardly making enough money to pay my rent and bills, much less the tuition for a private college. My parents always warned me to maintain my purity.

But you know what? Screw them. Because I need money, and fast. If my virginity is truly so valuable, then it should be worth some decent cash, too, right?

Luckily, the bidders on my online auction seem to agree with me on that. In fact, two of them have been sending me gifts to try and woo me, even outside of the bidding war itself. All I know are their usernames: ATurner97 and SaulHackzxx. That's what they go by on MyCampusList, and those are the names on the gifts I've been receiving. So far, they have sent me cute lingerie and shoes in my exact size, thigh-high stockings, expensive perfumes and makeup, flowers, teddy bears, even gift cards to fancy restaurants in town. I guess they want me to know they have the money to spend on me. One of them sent me this bra, and the other sent me these panties.

I think about my two mystery men while I touch myself, rolling my hips and sighing with pleasure as the tension builds up inside of me. I bite my lip to keep from moaning, afraid that my next-door neighbors will hear me. But when I finally cum, I can't help but cry out, gasping for air.

"Oh my gosh!" I whimper, feeling my pussy convulse with waves of indescribable pleasure. "Is *that* what it feels like?" I gasp, totally shocked. I lie there, breathing hard, staring up at the ceiling while my body comes down from the high. I never knew that an orgasm could feel like that. I assumed everyone was exaggerating about how good it feels. But oh my goodness, they were all so right!

Suddenly, I can't believe how crazy it is that I have waited so long. I've wasted so many years trying to be a good girl, avoiding this amazing, natural pleasure all this time. And for what? I have lost countless boyfriends who got tired of waiting. I never even kissed any of them. To think, all these years, I've been hiding from true pleasure, just because my parents say it's wrong. Something this fantastic simply cannot be wrong.

I sit up and look at the webpage. In an hour, the time limit on the auction will run out, and the winner will be selected. Whoever bids the most money will win the prize: my innocence. It feels so dirty and sexy that I can feel myself getting turned on all over again. Especially when I think to myself, well, if touching my own pussy felt that good, how much more amazing will it feel to have someone else touch me down there?

I can hardly wait to find out who will win. But I'm feeling antsy waiting around here, so I hop out of bed, shower off, get dressed in my usual modest long skirt and long-sleeved shirt, and pack up my stuff. I sling my backpack over my shoulder and make my way across campus to the courtyard. It's my favorite place to sit and study, in the sunshine and fresh air. I set up my laptop and blanket under a big tree. I curl up with my laptop, leaning back against the gnarled trunk, watching the people pass by as the minutes tick away on the auction.

So many hot guys walk past me, some of them turning to smile at me. I demurely tuck a ringlet of my auburn hair behind my ear and bite my lip, looking away. I can feel my cheeks blushing pink, just from their attention. It doesn't take much to fluster me. I've never even had a long conversation with a boy. I tend to steer clear of them. Even the boys I dated in high school learned quickly to keep their hands to themselves. We went on chaperoned dates at diners and movies, with at least one strict parent sitting right next to us, watching our hands like a hawk. No touching. No overt flirting. Even the few times I sneaked out to meet up with a boy, I never let him touch me. My shame and fear went that deep.

But not anymore. Now that I'm on my own, now that I've felt what an orgasm feels like, all I want to do is sleep with every guy I see. I wonder if any of them are the bidders in my auction. It turns me on to think that any one of these young men could be my potential first time. I look down at the screen and my heart skips a beat: there's only twenty seconds left!

The number has picked up, but the two remaining bidders keep punching the number incrementally higher, trying to outdo each other. I hold my breath as the countdown comes to an end. The screen reloads… to reveal that it's a tie! Both guys have bid the exact same amount in the last second! I cover my mouth in surprise, not sure what to do. I scroll down to see a conversation happening between ATurner97 and SaulHackzxx in the comments. My two winners, discussing how to handle the situation. How to handle *me*.

I watch as they come to a conclusion: that both men will meet up with me. Both men will compete with each other, in person, to see who gets to take my virginity. I will be blindfolded, not knowing who is who, and they will each do their best to give me pleasure and make me cum. Whoever wins, gets the prize: my virginity. I can't believe how civil they are, both of them discussing my virginity so pragmatically, like it's just a simple little commodity. And yet, they seem to show a level of respect toward me that I never would have guessed. I'm starting to think that all those years of my parents warning me about how evil and dangerous boys are, they were flat-out lying to me! They always made boys sound so treacherous, but if this is what they're like, then what's the problem?

Smiling excitedly, I post a comment in response to them:

Hi boys! Congratulations on being the winners. I agree to your deal. How about we all three meet at the Saguaro Motel out on Highway 89 on Friday night at 8 PM? I will provide the blindfold, myself. ;)

I click 'send' and wait impatiently for them to respond. I let out a little squeal of delight when they both agree to my plan. It's really happening!

~

It's Friday night, and my stomach is a-flutter with butterflies. I'm so nervous and excited I have hardly been able to sleep, just lying awake at night, imagining what is in store for me when I finally meet up with my two mystery guys. I can't wait to see what they look like, what they sound like. Of course, I won't get to know what they look like at first. You know, with the whole blindfold thing.

That makes me a little nervous as I drive out away from town, rolling down the dusty desert highway toward the Saguaro Motel. Admittedly, it's kind of a shady place, I suppose. I know it from whispers of gossip, about how it's known as a honeymooning spot for couples who just had shotgun weddings. It's the kind of pastel-pink and turquoise desert oasis that is clean and safe, but hasn't been upgraded or redecorated since the early '90s. None of that bothers me much, though, as I walk up to the front desk and ask for a room. What matters to me, the reason why I selected this motel in particular, is that it's out of town. Away from campus. Away from any potentially prying eyes, people who could judge me in whispers. Even though I'm partly doing this to stick it to my conservative, uptight parents, I still don't exactly want them to find out. Not yet, anyway. If I ever tell them-- and that's a big if-- it'll be on my terms. Not because some snobby, nosy busybody decides to tell them for me.

I know for a fact my parents have little spies on campus. Heck, that's how they found out that I went to that frat party a few weekends ago! Someone must have been watching me, and tattletaling back to my parents in the small town where they still live. The last thing I need is another scandal that will send ripples of rumors and judgement through my hometown. Although, the longer I spend at Marysvale, the less I ever want to return to my hometown. I prefer being a face in a crowd, the anonymity of campus. I feel like a grown-up, finally, and not just some innocent little girl being led around by her mommy and daddy.

I check into my hotel room and post the room number to the MyCampusList page for my auction, commenting in the posts below. I wait for a response, and it comes moments later. My two mystery guys will be here soon.

"Oh goodness," I gasp, feeling the jitters all over again. I hurriedly rush to put on the sexy, lacy baby pink lingerie my two winning bidders sent me. I rush into the bathroom to put some finishing touches on my hair and makeup. I've spent the week trolling through Youtube videos of makeup artists teaching how to do simple smokey eyes and less dramatic nighttime looks. I have never worn makeup before. My parents told me it was sinful. Inviting temptation. But now? Who cares what they think! I look good. And what's more, I *feel* good. I've also done up my hair in pretty curls, cascading down my shoulders. I smile in the reflection, my light smattering of freckles and dimples making me look young and innocent, in sharp contrast to the sexy get-up I'm wearing. I wonder how old my bidders are. But I hardly have the time to think too much about it before there's a knock at the door!

I hurry out of the bathroom and nervously smooth down the sheets, fluffing the pillows on the bed. Then I rush to the door and unlock it. In my haste, I nearly forget all about our plan, but then a deep male voice says, "Wait. Remember the blindfold. Go sit on the bed and put the blindfold on. We will come in when your eyes are safely covered."

"Oh. Right. Of course," I say quickly. Apart from teaching myself how to do makeup, I have also taken a couple visits to a local sex shop, to pick out some items that might aid me in my upcoming double date. Among the items are restraints, handcuffs, lube, a vibrator, and a paddle for spanking. And of course, the required blindfold. I'm not one-hundred-percent sure how to use these things, but I want to be prepared.

So I tie the blindfold tightly around my head and sit down on the edge of the springy bed, folding my hands neatly in my lap. I take a deep breath and call out: "I'm ready."

The door creaks open and two pairs of heavy footsteps cross the room, approaching me slowly. I'm breathing hard, my heart racing a million miles a second. I wish I could see their faces, their bodies. It's scary not knowing what's about to happen, even though it's exciting, too.

"H-How do you guys want to do this?" I ask anxiously.

Both men chuckle good-naturedly. Suddenly, there's a large hand holding each of my own. The man to my left raises my hand to his lips and kisses it gently, saying, "I'm Alex."

The man to my right lifts my other hand and kisses it. He says in a raspier voice than the first, "I'm Saul. Good to finally meet you."

I smile and blush. "My name is Lucy. But I guess you guys already knew that."

"Don't be scared," says the man to my left, Alex. "We're going to take good care of you. The whole reason I joined the bidding was to make sure your first time was worthwhile. I didn't want any weirdos to go after you."

There's another chuckle, and the other man, Saul

speaks up. "And me? I'm the weirdo. But don't worry, I won't hurt you. Not too much."

"This is a competition. To see who makes you feel the best. So, keep count of your orgasms. Make mental notes. Compare and contrast," says Alex.

"But above all, relax. Enjoy the ride, baby," says Saul.

I giggle nervously. "Okay. So, who's going to go first?"

Suddenly, one of the men sweeps me up into his arms. I squeal with surprise and delight as he stands me up. He walks over to the bed behind me and comes back to pin my arms behind my back. He clinks the cool metal of the handcuffs around my wrists, binding me. I'm admittedly a little frightened, but I'm aroused, too. I've never been bound like this before, even in my wildest dreams. Then Saul leads me over to stand in front of him as he sits down on the edge of the bed. I can feel him pull me down over his lap, my ass sticking up in the air. The next thing I know, there's a *THWAP* and then a smack of searing pain against my ass. I cry out in shock and pain, but when the initial sting melts away, all I feel is pleasure. He spanks me again and again, undoubtedly leaving bright marks on my skin.

"Oh my gosh," I whimper. Saul strokes my hair,

feeling me up, groping my ass and breasts as I'm bent over his lap.

"Bet you never expected that, hmm? But you know, it's such a dirty thing for a sweet, innocent girl to do: sell off her virginity. I think you need a little punishment," Saul growls.

He smacks my ass again, this time with the palm of his hand. I let out a little moan, surprised at myself. It's perverse and strange, but the punishment actually turns me on. He's squeezing my tits, sliding his rough hands over my soft, virgin skin.

"Soft and perfect," he purrs. "Like a porcelain doll. You're beautiful, you know that? I can't believe no man has touched this gorgeous body. A girl like you doesn't come along very often. You're special. I can tell. I used to walk by you in the courtyard, watch you sitting on a blanket under that big tree. So studious and sweet. Innocent. I used to daydream about spreading you out on that blanket and fucking you 'til you screamed."

I gasp, not used to this kind of talk. I wrack my brain, trying to remember the faces of the many, many guys who walked past me in the courtyard. I wish I had paid more attention.

"I knew the moment I found your ad, I had to have you. I want to be the one to make you cum like crazy. I want to make you tremble and shake, Lucy. I'll be rough, but it'll feel good, I promise. Does that sound good to you?" he asks softly.

"Yes. Yes, please," I whisper back.

"Good girl," he grunts. He stands me up again and then lowers me back down to sit on his lap facing away from him. He wraps his big, strong arms around me, caressing my breasts, rolling my perky nipples between his fingers until I'm moaning and shivering with delight. Then he spread my legs wide open and began to rub my clit through the lace of my panties.

"I love seeing you in these panties," he hisses in my ear. "So fucking sexy."

He kisses my neck, softly at first, then harder, grazing my sensitive skin with his teeth just enough to send shivers of pleasure down my spine. His left hand squeezes my breasts, groping me and toying with my nipples, while his right hand rubs faster and harder against my clit. It's not long before I'm cumming, with a shout of bliss.

"Oh-- goodness!" I cry out, gushing through my panties.

"Oh, very good. Very good," he purrs. He reaches back for something, moving away just long enough to grab something from the little pile of items on the bed. There's a mechanical whirring noise, and then I'm overcome with stimulation as Saul turns the vibrator up to the highest setting and presses it hard against my over-sensitized clit. I wriggle and writhe under the intense sensation, moaning and whimpering. I can't decide if it feels amazing or if it hurts-- I think maybe it's both.

"Feel good, Lucy?" he growls, rubbing the head of the vibrator in tight circles around my clit. Explosions of pleasure wrack my whole body, making it difficult to think, much less speak.

"Y-Yes," I manage to choke out, riding the waves of powerful sensations as Saul gropes me lewdly, sucking bruises into my neck and punishing my clit with the vibrator. I shudder and whine as another orgasm rips through me.

"Fuck yes," he hisses. "Cum for me again, baby."

He bites the soft flesh of my neck and presses the vibrator harder on my clit. I'm seeing stars, my heart racing as I struggle to stay coherent. It's all too much. It's almost violent, the way he manhandles me, the way he manipulates my trembling little cunny. I cum again, whimpering and shaking. If not for his powerful grip, I might collapse off of his lap. Saul lets go of me and I sigh, both in relief and disappointment.

"On your knees," he orders. I obey quickly, feeling my way around to kneel in front of him. A moment later, I hear a zipper being tugged down and something hard and huge being pressed against my lips. Instinctively, I open my mouth, and he shoves his cock down my throat.

I let out a little yelp of surprise, choking a little. Saul strokes my hair back out of my face, caressing and calming me as I slowly relax my jaw and begin to warm to the feeling of a gigantic dick in my mouth. I reach up to stroke his length while I lick the head of his cock, reveling in the velvety softness of his skin, the intoxicatingly musky scent, the massive size. He gives me a few moments to get acquainted before pushing his cock all the way inside my mouth, brushing against the back of my throat until I'm nearly gagging. But oddly enough, it doesn't bother me. In fact, I can feel my pussy getting wetter by the second as I devour his cock, bobbing up and down and gaining confidence. Saul is groaning, rutting into my throat.

"Fuck, what a dirty little mouth," he hisses, stroking my hair as I blow him. "But this isn't just about my cock. No. I want to make that little pussy purr. Stand up."

I obey quickly and he guides me over to the bed,

cradling me back until my head touches the pillows. I lie there in anticipation, waiting to see what he does next. Then I feel the pressure of a heavier body on the bed, moving closer. Again, he brushes his cock against my lips and I open them gladly, sucking him off with enthusiasm. Only now I realize that he's facing the other way, leaning over me. As I suck his cock, I hear the vibrator turn on again, and a moment later the head of it is pressed against my pussy again. I shudder and moan, rocking my hips as he rips the panties off of me, tossing them aside to get at my bare, sensitive clit. He pushes down hard while I moan and whimper around his cock, letting him fuck my throat while my pleasure mounts higher and higher.

I cum again and again, whining and writhing under the merciless vibrations, soaking the bed sheets underneath me. "Fuck yes," Saul growls. "Get that tight little cunt soaking wet."

He takes his cock out of my mouth and moves down the bed. I hear the sound of a bottle being popped open, and a squirt of something liquid. The lube. Still pressing the vibe to my clit, he rubs a little circle around my asshole. I shy away, recoiling a little at first. I have no idea why he would ever put his fingers there. That's not how it works, right?

"Shh, it's okay, baby. I won't hurt you. I promise, this'll feel good," Saul assures me. I relax a little, still squirming as my pussy erupts with another orgasm. Slowly, methodically, Saul manages to work his finger inside my ass, gently fingering me while the vibrator pleasures my sensitive clit. I let out a long, awestruck squeal at how good it feels.

"Mhm. That's right, Lucy. I knew you'd love it," he growls. "You like it in the ass, don't you, angel?"

"Yes. Oh goodness, yes," I murmur, tossing from side to side as the waves of bliss rattle through me. He continues on for awhile, making me cum again and again.

Finally, I hear another male voice. "Come on. My turn, man."

It's Alex, who has been politely quiet this entire time. "Alright. Fair enough," Saul says. "Remember, it's all about her."

"I think I can handle this," Alex replies confidently. The vibrator is turned off and Saul steps away, leaving me lying there overwhelmed and on fire, wondering what to expect next. Alex approaches, sitting softly on the bed beside me. He crooks a strong arm underneath me, lifting me enough to open the handcuffs. He tosses them aside and lets me stretch a little, feeling the ache in my arms and sting in my wrists. Then he gently lifts my hands to his lips and kisses my wrists, as though kissing the pain away. It's such an incredibly sweet gesture that I can feel my heart almost melting.

His hands come up to caress my face, holding me gently, like I'm something fragile and delicate. Something truly precious. He strokes my hair, leaning in to softly brush his lips against mine. I open my mouth, leaning into him eagerly. He cups my cheek while he kisses me, gently probing his tongue into my mouth while he reaches around to my back, to unclasp my bra. It falls away easily, my breasts free and exposed to the cool air. I moan into Alex's mouth as he kisses me, his hands moving down my neck, over my collarbone, down my chest, to delicately fondle my breasts. The feeling of his warm hands on my sensitive skin makes me shiver with delight. He strokes soft circles around both of my nipples, rhythmically circling with perfect symmetry, until I'm whimpering and weak.

After Saul's rough manhandling, there's something especially comforting about the way Alex seems to worship my body. Not a single inch of my body goes untouched. He runs his hands down the length of my arms, thumbing over my fingers delicately. For a moment he interlaces his fingers with mine as we kiss, which warms my heart. He's giving me all kinds of butterflies. He moves to sit behind me, kissing my neck softly while he kneads the tension out of my shoulders. I sigh and lean back against him, losing myself to the soothing pressure.

"You really are beautiful," he says, his voice ticklish against the shell of my ear. "I knew it from the moment I saw you, I would never meet another girl like you. I still believe that. Nobody could convince me otherwise."

"You've seen me before?" I ask, suddenly very curious. "Have we met?"

He sighs, another puff of ticklishness that makes me tremble deliciously. "No. I saw you across a very crowded room. There were people everywhere. Dancing. Drinking. Fooling around. Girls everywhere, and then... you. Standing in the corner, holding a cup of water. I knew it was water. I could just tell that you were too afraid to drink like everyone else. Too cautious."

I flash back to the frat party a few weekends back. "The party at the Sigma Nu house," I whisper, stunned to know he was there.

"Yes. I wish I could have gone up and talked to you, but you looked content to stay close by to your classmates. I didn't want to interrupt," Alex explains.

"You should have," I confess. "I-I think I would have liked to meet you."

Alex gets up and gently pulls me to the middle of the bed. He grabs my ankles in his hands and says calmly, "I'm going to tie you up. Don't worry. I'll make it feel good."

"Okay," I murmur. "I trust you."

I can almost feel Saul rolling his eyes from across the room. It's obvious that my two suitors have two very distinct styles. It's hard to say which one I prefer. In fact, I think perhaps they compliment each other well.

Alex binds my ankles loosely to the bed posts at the end of the bed, spreading my legs wide open in the process. I was a ballerina growing up, so my residual flexibility makes it easy enough to do this. I have no doubts that Alex would stop if I told him to. But I want to know what he has planned. He climbs back onto the bed, weighing down the mattress between my legs. I hold my breath, anticipating his next move.

Then I shudder and sigh with pleasure as I feel his warm, wet tongue licking along the length of my slick flower. He grabs my thighs, massaging the muscles there and loosening me up while he devours my pussy. He licks at my clit, suckling it and making me moan with delight. It's a different kind of plea-sure from the overbearing intensity of the vibrator. Softer, more relaxing. Comforting, almost. Alex settles into a rhythm, licking up and down, circling my clit until I can feel tears burning in my eyes. It feels so good, every muscle in my body pleasantly tensed. Then, I'm overwhelmed with bliss when he slips a finger inside my pussy.

"Ohhh my gosh," I mumble, biting my lip. "Oh, it feels so good."

He hooks the end of his finger, stroking expertly at the deep, hidden hub of sensitivity inside of me. It feels almost too good to be true. Alex moans as he eats me out, sending wonderful vibrations up through my body. Before long, I'm rolling my hips, gently thrusting up to meet his tongue, his finger gently stroking that place deep within me. It takes me a little longer to ramp up to a climax, but when I get there, it's mindblowing.

I let out a little yelp as I gush cum all over Alex's hand and lips. He eagerly, hungrily laps up my honey, moaning as he picks up the pace. He doesn't let up for a single second, and I can do nothing but hold on and ride the wave. Orgasm after orgasm rolls through me, my body convulsing and trembling every time. Alex plays my cunny like a finely-tuned instrument, like it's the most natural thing in the world for him. I nearly lose count of the times I cum onto his face, my mind floating elsewhere on cloud nine.

When it all becomes too overwhelming, I start to instinctively pull away, and Alex stops immediately. I can hear him lick his fingers, getting every last drop of my cum. Then he says softly, "Let's give your pussy a little break, shall we? You want a cock in that pretty little mouth? Hmm?"

I nod vigorously. "Oh, yes. Please," I beg him. He moves up the bed, pulling me up to sit as he kneels in front of me. He guides me to his cock and I tug it into my mouth with a moan of pleasure. It turns me on to have a dick in my mouth. I never expected that. But something about yet another one of my holes being filled with thick cock... just makes me wetter than ever.

Alex starts out slow, pulling back and cautiously thrusting into my mouth. But then I reach up and start to fondle his balls and stroke his thick, hard length while I pump him in and out of my mouth, and he gives in. "Oh, fuck. God, that mouth feels so good, Lucy," he groans.

He pulls my hair back, gently using it to guide me, pressuring me to take him deeper and deeper into my mouth until it touches the back of my throat. I swirl my tongue around the engorged head, flicking it along the underside of his cock, until he's almost losing control. Alex fucks my mouth, groaning through gritted teeth. I can tell it's bringing him closer and closer to cumming, and I'm half-intending to get him all the way there. I just love the taste of him in my mouth. But before he can lose it, he softly pushes me back, then straddles me. At first, I suck in a deep breath, thinking he's about to put his cock inside my cunt. But instead, he kisses me passionately, pressing the head of his cock against my folds, rubbing it up and down, over my clit and back down and up again. It feels surprisingly amazing, and it's not long before I'm cumming again and again, moaning into his kiss.

"Please," I beg him when we break apart for a gasp of air. "I want you to fuck me. I need a cock inside me. Now."

I can tell Alex wants to go ahead, but instead he backs away, leaving me sitting on the bed desperate and pouting. I hear Saul's voice, saying, "Well, I think it's time to take the blindfold off, but first, you have to tell us who gave you more pleasure. Who wins?"

I think it over for a moment, weighing both options against each other. Then, finally, I confess to them, "I can't choose. You both made me cum the same amount. It's a tie… again."

"What should we do then?" Saul asks.

"Yeah, it's all about you. What do you want, Lucy?" Alex asks.

An idea occurs to me. I slip the blindfold off and look at the two handsome men in front of me for the first time. Alex is lanky and lean, with dark hair, soft brown eyes, and a pair of black-rimmed glasses. He gives me a reassuring smile. Saul is broad-shouldered, a little thicker, with dark blond curls and green eyes. He regards me with the hungry eyes of a wolf.

"I want you both to fuck me," I answer. I look at Saul. "You put your finger in my… um. Can you do that again? But this time, I want your cock."

I glance over at Alex and tell him, "And you. I want you to fuck my pussy. A virgin hole for each of you. Fair enough?"

Both men agree wholeheartedly. And within seconds, they're on top of me, overwhelming me with touches and kisses. Four hands roving down my body, feeling me up, groping and fondling me in a confusion of crazed desire. They kiss me, move me around, slap my ass. Lube is squirted onto fingers, rubbing and fingering both my tight little holes. Saul thrusts two fingers inside my ass while Alex uses the vibrator on my clit, making me cum over and over. Then, with my legs still bound to the bed posts, Saul maneuvers himself underneath me and slowly pushes his cock inside my ass. I whimper and shiver with mingled pain and pleasure.

"Oh gosh. It's so big," I gasp.

"I know, baby. But it feels good, doesn't it?" Saul growls in my ear. I nod.

"Yes. Oh gosh, yes," I reply breathlessly as he begins to thrust up into me, grabbing onto my hips to hold me steady. I reach up for Alex, who straddles me and gives me reassuring kisses while he gently, carefully slides his massive cock inside my aching, virginal cunny.

"Alex," I whisper, clinging to him for dear life as both men pick up the pace, fucking my ass and my tight little pussy at the same time. The sensation of two cocks inside me is almost too much. Sensory overload. I cum over and over, dripping my honey all over their cocks as they slam into me, shattering my virginity, stealing every drop of my innocence. They fuck me harder and faster until I'm spasming with pleasure, and just when I think I can't take anymore, Alex and Saul cum inside me within moments of each other, groaning and showering me in kisses from behind and the front. All three of us collapse in an overwhelmed pile of heaving chests and sticky bodies, with me in the middle.

Once we clean ourselves up, they pay me the amount promised. But before they leave, I tell them shyly, "If you ever wanted to do this again... I'd do it for free."

One year later, I can safely say that I am the happiest I've ever been. I'm sitting in the living room of the fancy apartment I share with my two loves, nursing our three-month old daughter, Lily. I'm watching as Saul drinks a beer and builds a new TV stand on the rug in front of me. He has a rugged charm, the way he uses his strength and mechanical mind to put it together. Alex comes walking over with a tray of snacks and a glass of sparkling grape juice to go with his wine. It almost makes me laugh to see our wildly different choices. Saul's beer, Alex's wine, my grape juice. But it's the variety among us that makes it work so well. My boys have started a computer science company together. As it turns out, that's how they know each other: from classes. Alex is a programmer, and Saul?

Well, he's been a hacker for years. Of course, now that he has Alex and I in his life, and the baby, he only uses his powers for good.

And damn, is it so good. It's hard being a full time student and a mom, but I wouldn't trade my life for anything in the world. I live in a little bubble of love, and I never want to leave.

BONUS

If you sign up for my mailing list, you'll get updates on my new books, bundles, giveaways **and**, for a limited time, a **Free, exclusive** book: Twin Passions. This story isn't available anywhere else except to my newsletter, and contains sexy, taboo content.

All you have to do to read this full length novella is visit http://candyquinn.com/newsletter to get your instant, **free** access to this exclusive & sexy story!

Sign up & get 4 Taboo Books FREE
from Amazon Bestselling erotica author
CANDY QUINN

ABOUT THE AUTHOR

Candy Quinn loves writing naughty, dirty stories - both short and sexy, and long and scandalous. Lots of taboo pregnancy, discipline, and first time virgins fill her filthy mind, which she loves to share with you. If you need something to scratch that secret itch, turn to Candy!

facebook.com/candyquinn
twitter.com/sexycandyquinn
bookbub.com/authors/candy-quinn

ALSO BY CANDY QUINN

Breeding Erotica - On The Farm

Nympho Farm Girl

The Farmgirl & The Fugitive: A Fertile First Time

Dixie: Fertile First Time on the Farm

Bought by the Billionaire

The Farmgirl & The Bandit

The Military Man and the Farmgirl

Breeding Erotica - Bad Boys

Bought by the Bad Boy

Fertile First Time with a Bad Boy Biker: The Farmgirl &
The Outlaw

Dancing for the Mob Boss

Shipwrecked Beauty: Lost in Lust

Breeding Erotica - Virgins

Fertile Bookworm

Making Sweet Music

Exposed

Sweet on Her Boss

Rory: Off Limits

Breeding Erotica - Other

Playing His Princess

Parked Between Her Thighs

Tease

Bad Seed

The Bet

The Fertile Stewardess: Mile High with a Billionaire

His Fertile Sweetheart: Bareback High School Reunion

His Fertile Present - FMF

Love that First Night

The Fertile Tour Guide

And a Fertile New Year

The Fertile Bride

The Fertile Beauty Queen

The Fertile Beauty Queen & My Wife

The Doctor and the Fertile Housewife

The Doctor and the Fertile Housewives

His Fertile Groupie

Desperate For It

Step Erotica

Taboo Passions: Emma & Brody

Cam Girl for the Man of the House

Stepbrother's Baby

Taboo Threesome (FFM)

Pregnant Brat for Christmas

The Priest's Brat

Teaching the Brat

Forbidden Angel: Taboo M/F/M Erotica

His Brat's Fertile First Time: Blaire: A Taboo Bareback

His Brat's Fertile First Time - Avril: Taboo

The Billionaire & His Brat: A Taboo First Time

Other Erotica

Tending to His Fantasies

Matchmaker

Bombshell

World's Finest

Discipline the Dancer

Romance Novellas

Stranded Beauty

Dirty Country Love

The Fugitive: A Romance Novella

Innocent Farm Girl: An E-Romance Novella

Precious Pet: A Billionaire BDSM E-Romance

Sharing Her Series (MFM Breeding)

Buying Her

Catering to Her

Exhibitionist For Her

Teaching Her

Rocking Her

Trading for Her

Stealing Her

Awakening Her

Punishing Her

Blindfolding Her

Nympho - Amber

The Nympho

The Nympho Halloween

Nympho off the Pill

Nympho for the Gang

Nympho Angel

Nympho Valentine

Sugar Daddies Series

Karen's Sugar Daddy

Christine's Sugar Daddies

Olivia's Sugar Daddy

Sugar Daddy Rock Star

The Delaney Brothers (Billionaire Romance)

Alastair

William

Tristian

Jack

Taboo Passions: Sylvia & Zach (Taboo First Time)

Book 1

Book 2

Book 3

Taboo Passions: Cole & Mackenzie (Taboo Breeding)

Book 1

Book 2

Book 3

The Fertile Farm Series (Breeding)

Daisy

Lucy

Rosa

Mandy - Part 1

Mandy - Part 2

Mandy - Part 3

Fertile First Time Series (Virgin MFM)

Her Fertile First Time (Also in Audiobook)

Her Fertile Second Time

Lynn's Fertile First Time

Katie's Fertile First Time

Becca's Fertile First Time

First Time College Gangbang (Virgin MFMMM)

Fertile Cheerleader

Fertile Sorority

Fertile Birthday

Fertile Freshman for the Team

The Innocent Tease Series (Breeding)

The Student: Punished by the Priest: #1

The Student: Pleasured by Her Older Friend: #2

The Student: Seducing The Mayor: #3

The Student: Pleasing Her Professor: #4

Biker's Sugar Babe Series (Multiple Partners)

Taken by the Bar: Biker's Sugar Babe (Part 1)

Claimed by the Biker: Biker's Sugar Babe (Part 2)

Taken by the Biker's Gang: Biker's Sugar Babe (Part 3)

Arrested by the Sexy Cop: Biker's Sugar Babe (Part 4)

Sugar Baby (Breeding)

Paige

Claimed by the Bad Boy Biker Series (Breeding)

Book 1

Book 2

Book 3

Laura's Innocence Series (Breeding)

Book 1

Book 2

Anthologies

Forbidden Fertile Brats 1

Too Taboo! 3: A Forbidden Fun Taboo Bundle

Forbidden Fantasies (A Naughty List Taboo Collection)

All for One and One for All 3 (The Naughty List Menage Boxed Set)

50 Forbidden Fantasies

Sting of Lust: 20 Book BDSM Domination Romance Mega Bundle (Excite Spice Boxed Sets)

No Shame in Submission (Shameless Book Bundles 7)

I Love It: 10 Intense Stories to Keep the Passion Alive (Shameless Book Bundles 6)

Hopelessly Outnumbered: 10 Stories. 53 Men. 13 Women. You Do The Math (Shameless Book Bundles)

Take the Heat: A Criminal Romance Anthology

Club Alpha: BDSM Romance Boxed Set

Shades of Surrender: Fifty by Fifty #4: A Billionaire

Romance Boxed Set

So Wrong 8: The Ultimate Taboo Box Set

Anything for the Man of the House: Ten Brats who Learn
how to Behave (Shameless Book Bundles 5)

GET MORE ROMANCE & EROTICA
HERE

The Naughty List.
  Shameless Book Deals.
  Excite Spice.